Lethal ADHESION

DOBI CROSS

Luxhaven
Publishing

ISBN paperback, 978-1-958987-12-4

Interior & Cover Design by Luxhaven Publishing

Editing by JD Book Services

Proofreading by Lisa Lee Proofreading

To JC, Grandma D, and DC, whom I love more than life itself.

READ MORE BY DOBI CROSS

Dr. Zora Smyth Medical Thriller Series

Lethal Emergency (Prequel)

Lethal Dissection

Lethal Incision

Lethal Obsession

Lethal Reconciliation

Lethal Adhesion

Lethal Retraction

SEE ALL OF DOBI CROSS BOOKS

at https://dobicross.com

Thank you for choosing LETHAL ADHESION. Zora Smyth was a character that I was fortunate to meet about a year ago as I brainstormed ideas for my first medical thriller story for an anthology.

LETHAL ADHESION continues the story of Zora Smyth as she prepares for her board exams and deals with an antagonistic colleague, a boyfriend who may not be who he says he is, and a new relationship with her sister. We see how Zora remains true to doing the best for her patients and believing in herself while keeping trust with her friends and family.

It was important for me as I penned this series to have Zora Smyth not be some super hero or a person with extraordinary abilities, but an everyday person who through the journey of the next few books comes to fully understand and appreciate who she truly is and is able to heal from the childhood baggage she's carried all her life.

Please continue this journey with me in LETHAL RETRACTION. You can grab your copy at https://dobicross.com.

Would you also want to be notified when the next Dobi Cross book releases? Sign up at https://dobi-cross.com.

Once again, thank you so much for purchasing LETHAL ADHESION and for meeting Zora Smyth. If you enjoyed it, please consider leaving a review at your favorite retailer or recommending it to a friend.

Thanks again for your support!

Dobi Cross

Lethal
ADHESION

SIX MONTHS EARLIER

Alisa Smyth froze, and the words she'd planned to say stuck at the back of her throat, as she stared in horror at the man striding toward her with a tray of drinks. *It can't be,* her mind reasoned. Her thoughts scrambled to understand. *No, not with my beautiful, sweet sister. Not with my new family.*

But the nightmare kept unfolding in front of her like a terrible movie. "And this is Dave McKesson, my boyfriend," her sister, Zora, said to Alisa, her voice sounding muffled like Alisa's ears had filled with water.

Alisa shook her head and blinked, but she couldn't move. Her feet seemed anchored on the floor like they'd grown roots on the spot. Here she was, this wonderful fall afternoon at her family home, thinking she'd left everything about the criminal world behind, yet the nightmare seemed to have followed her here. No, it seemed hell had come ahead of her and made its home here to let her know it had her in its grasp and could never escape from it, ever. But maybe Alisa was dreaming and only had to wake up to get back to the 'welcome home' party her wonderful doctor of a sister and her family had organized for her.

She dug her fingernails into her palm, the sharp pain jolting all the way through her forearm, but the vision in front of Alisa didn't change. The last man she'd expected to see was standing in front of her, grinning like a Cheshire cat. He dropped the tray in his hands on the coffee table and then straightened. Alisa wasn't a violent person, but in that moment she wished she had a rock to smash the grin off the face of the man whose name was surely not Dave, a man who was not who he said he was.

Get a grip on yourself, Alisa. She couldn't fall apart, not here and not now. This was the first time she'd spent time with her long-lost family and friends since her kidnap many years ago, and Alisa couldn't let their first impression of her be one of paranoia and horror. No, she wouldn't let him ruin her new life, the life that was rightfully hers.

She took a deep breath to slow down her fast beating heart. She could do this.

"You okay, honey?" her mom asked, giving her a quizzical look.

Alisa flashed a forced smile she hoped would satisfy her. "I'm fine." Then she swung her eyes back to Dave. "I'm Alisa," she said, a mask of indifference now settling over her features.

"Nice to meet you," Dave said with a smile, and extended his hand.

Alisa looked down at it. A beautiful, manly hand, but one that had carried out cruel horrors.

She was loath to touch it, but everyone was watching, so she accepted the handshake for a second and not a moment longer. "Hello," she responded.

His hand had warmed her skin, yet Alisa fought the urge to wipe her hand clean. She watched as Zora looped her arm through Dave's. It took everything in Alisa not to rip her sister's arm away.

"I'm glad you're reunited with Zora," Dave said to Alisa. "Welcome back home."

And I'm not glad you're in it, Alisa thought. *I wish you were nowhere near her.* She needed to warn

Zora about him before her sister made a decision she'd regret.

Before she could ponder how to break the news to Zora, her mom grabbed Alisa's arm. "Come and tell me everything about how you're doing," she said.

Alisa allowed herself to be led away to the large brown leather sofa in the formal living room, but her thoughts were still on Dave. Maybe she could talk to Zora after the party—telling her right now in his presence would only alert Dave. All Alisa needed to do was tolerate him until the party ended. That didn't seem like such an impossible feat, right?

So she chatted and laughed with her mom and the other friends who were there for the occasion. But her eyes kept straying to where Dave sat with Zora, laughing and touching her like she meant the world to him. *Ugh*. Lies, all lies.

Soon, Alisa couldn't stand his presence any longer and got up to grab some hors d'oeuvres from the dining area. She picked up a small piece of tomato bruschetta and popped it into her mouth, but it tasted sour and ashy. She tried a different appetizer— it wasn't any better. It seemed Dave's presence had ruined even her taste buds. Giving up, she turned and stared at the happy couple across the room.

"I'm happy for her," a voice said from beside her.

Alisa turned to see Zora's bosom friend, Christina, reaching for a piece of spiced shrimp. "She's been through so much," she finished.

"What do you mean?" Alisa asked.

"She's been kidnapped, arrested, jailed, fired, and threatened at gunpoint. Then she lost a dear friend, Marcus, who was like a brother to her. That's too much life experience for someone who's only interested in saving patients. And then you were missing for so long. You could tell she'd lost a big piece of her heart. And now you're back, and he's back in her life! Zora has never been happier. See, she's glowing."

"What do you mean, he's back?"

"Oh, Zora and Dave dated in high school. Then you went missing, and Zora pushed everyone away from her life, including him. She dated no one else after that. Thank goodness he's here for her now. They were always good together. She'd be devastated if anything happened to him."

A headache pounded at the back of Alisa's head, and she rubbed her neck to ease it. This was terrible and only made things more complicated. It seemed telling Zora the truth would shatter what little happiness she had, yet how could Alisa keep something like this from her?

She glanced at the couple again and watched as Zora nestled her head against Dave's chest. The look of pure joy on her face was unmistakable. Alisa's heart ached at the thought of taking that away from Zora, yet she couldn't hide the truth. But if Dave meant so much to Zora, then Alisa needed more concrete evidence and not mere speculations before she tried to convince Zora of his true identity.

In the meantime, Alisa would wait while keeping an eye on him.

Until she had everything she needed.

P RESENT DAY
Lucas Prachette's nostrils flared so hard it seemed smoke was about to blast from them. Who would have thought the black-and-white photo in the newspaper clipping he held would send blood roaring through his veins?

The muscles in his jaw tightened. He'd heard the rumors but hadn't wanted to believe them. Yet the clipping was evidence enough. The man who stared back at him from the picture featured on it was everything he loathed. *Betrayer. Traitor. Murderer.* The worst of his kind. He deserved everything that was coming to him.

Lucas folded the sheet of paper and slid it across to the boyish-looking figure sitting opposite him, a man who'd presented himself as his lawyer. It still surprised him the man had responded to the request he'd sent a few months ago. Lucas had waited and hoped, since they'd warned him the man was picky that way. Now it seemed it'd been worth it—this revenge wasn't one best served in a hurry.

His eyes swept across the room as the man studied the clipping. The room was as bland as ever with its crumbling cream paint job—most likely done by prisoners looking to earn favors. A mustard-colored couch that had seen better days hunched against one wall, while an ancient-looking desk with chipped corners that must have been handed down over the years from one warden to the next until it'd become a permanent fixture in the room sat close to the windows with two wood-framed visitors' chairs facing it.

A musty smell mixed with the faint scent of french fries hung in the air as if it'd been forever since they'd opened windows of this office. He hated being here instead of out in the fresh air, taking the run he enjoyed. Still, the opportunity to meet this man was worth more than the mid-day exercise period he'd had to miss.

The man adjusted his black-rimmed glasses as he nodded once, slid the newspaper clipping into the inner pocket of his expensive suit, picked up his briefcase, and left the room.

Lucas leaned back on the couch in relief. It was done. A deal had been struck, and the money would be wired, as usual, through a Swiss account. All Lucas had to do now was wait for the good news.

From what he'd heard, the boyish-looking man had never failed before, and he always kept his promises. His methods might have been atypical—one never knew what to expect with him—yet he always delivered without leaving clues behind that might hint that there was anything more to the deaths of his victims than natural causes.

A thin smile played on Lucas' lips as his fingers plucked a stray thread from his orange jumpsuit. It was time for the man in the photo to disappear. The one who seemed to have something going on with the doctor featured next to him in the clipping.

The man named Dave McKesson.

D ead. Dead. Dead.

Those were the words that raced through Dr. Zora Smyth's mind, in time with the constant blare from the cardiac monitor that dominated the air.

The muscles of her jaw tightened. *This shouldn't have happened*, she thought as she gazed down at the still body of the middle-aged male patient lying on a gurney in one of Lexinbridge Regional Hospital's Emergency Room cubicles. He should have had emergency surgery after they'd seen him in the ER— he'd have only needed a brief hospital stay before heading home. Maybe he could have even had a lobster roll for dinner in about a week. Now the patient was going to the morgue.

Zora let out a small sigh. This was what came from hiring idiots like Herbert IV into the general surgical residency program. Herbert—a fellow chief surgical resident of Zora's at the hospital—had no business working with patients. Why?

No empathy. Check.

Poor surgical skills. Check. He was a fifth-year resident, for goodness' sake. If he hadn't mastered the basics by now, when would he ever learn?

Incompetence. Check.

Zora had lost count of how many times other junior residents had taken the blame for Herbert's mistakes. And the list went on and on.

As far as Zora was concerned, a surgeon with all the above was a licensed murderer waiting to happen. Why was Herbert still in the program when any other doctor with his issues would have been booted a long time ago? How had he even made it into this surgical residency program that was so hard to get into in the first place? And no, she wasn't biased because Herbert had been best buddies with Dr. Graham, another colleague who'd been involved in a nasty organ trafficking case that Zora had blown open. Herbert had hated Zora long before that incident, for some unknown reason.

And where was the idiot, anyway? Herbert was

supposed to be on call and must have gotten the page about this patient. Thursday and Friday nights were busy days at the ER, so her department scheduled two senior residents on call on those days instead of one, which was how she'd ended up with him on the same call. Zora looked over the heads of the other medical staff in the cubicle who had worked hard to help resuscitate the patient and scanned for any signs of Herbert's hulking figure.

Nope. Still nowhere in sight.

Zora turned back to the patient. She couldn't leave yet—she had one more thing to do for him. "Time of death is nine twenty-one p.m." She stood aside and watched as they covered the patient with a pale blue hospital linen, while another nurse began dismantling the breathing apparatus. Then Zora stepped out of the cubicle to break the news to the family.

Fifteen minutes later, Zora reached the surgical residents' lounge and yanked open the door so hard it slammed against the wall behind it. A few heads in the room jerked in her direction at the sound, but Zora ignored them. Her eyes searched and then narrowed as she spied the person she was looking for.

Herbert sat at a workstation, his broad back to her and his concentration focused on the large burger he was scarfing down, ketchup dripping down the corners of his mouth.

Zora's hand closed into a fist. A patient was dead because of his incompetence, and he was eating a burger?

Herbert got up in that moment as he stretched to reach the box of tissues on the far corner of the workstation.

A sardonic smile crossed Zora's face. The universe was on her side.

She strode forward and wrenched Herbert's chair away as he made to sit down.

Herbert crashed on the floor with ketchup splattered all over him, his half-eaten burger landing in a mess a few feet away.

"What the… I'm going to sue you for assault!" Herbert screamed at Zora as he scrambled to his feet, his face a bright shade of red, and his neck strained with bulging veins.

"Assault? What assault?" a familiar voice said from a corner of the room.

Zora turned to see her best pal and fellow chief surgical resident, Brian Atkinson, step into view.

She crossed her arms over her chest. What was Brian doing here? He wasn't supposed to be on call tonight, but she was glad to see him all the same, and it felt good to have him back her up.

"Did anyone see an assault?" Brian asked, his voice echoing in the room. The other three residents in the space suddenly seemed more interested in whatever was in front of them. "I thought so." He shrugged and gave Herbert a lazy smile.

"You won't get away with this!" Herbert snarled as he tried to blot out the ketchup stains on his scrubs, to no avail. Instead, he grabbed his satchel from the workstation and stormed out of the room.

Zora winced at the sound of the slammed door that followed, and then felt some of her anger seep away. This was the most she could do to Herbert on behalf of the patient. Whatever happened next would depend on the hospital's mortality review process—if the case ever came under review.

Most of the cases that were examined were ones that presented an interesting teaching opportunity, were associated with a claim or lawsuit, or were tied to a sentinel event that the hospital deemed worthy to look into. Even the regular morbidity and mortality conferences were not enough to examine every single death in the department.

Brian strode to where Zora stood. "Are you okay?" he asked.

Zora cocked her head at the other residents. As if sensing her need for privacy, all three made their excuses and left the room. Zora's shoulders relaxed at the sound of the door closing behind her.

She nodded. "I know. You don't have to say it." She ran a hand over her pony-tailed hair. "I shouldn't have done that." She dropped into a nearby chair. "I was just…"

Brian patted her back and then settled into another chair close by. "It was long overdue. I heard about the patient. I'm sorry."

Zora arched an eyebrow at him. She sometimes marveled at how fast he got news from the hospital grapevine. "I don't know how you do it, Brian."

"What do you mean?"

"You somehow seem to know everything that's happening at the hospital. Teach me your ways."

Brian waved her away. "It's nothing. I stopped by the ER on my way in and heard about it from one of the nurses."

The image of the dead patient flashed through her mind again. Zora let out another heavy sigh and rubbed the back of her neck. "I don't know why he's still in the residency program. I never thought I'd meet a doctor this bad."

"Same."

"Why don't they do something? Anything? They can't say they haven't heard the rumors. There might have been some complaints, too."

"I don't know if any complaints against him exist, but you can't judge a doctor based on rumors alone."

"That doesn't mean you can't investigate them."

They both fell silent for a minute. The sound of the HVAC circulating fresh air through the room filled the air.

"Have you completed the mortality review form?" Brian asked. Any doctor whose patient had died in their care had to fill one out.

"Yes, and I clearly stated who his primary doctor was." The ER doctor had been the one to call Zora's attention to the patient when Herbert couldn't be reached.

"Then you've done the best you can," Brian said softly.

"What if this happens to another patient?"

"Zora, you know you can't control that. Besides, this is not the time to be a hero. Boards are around the corner."

Boards. How could she forget? She'd looked forward to the boards—the qualifying exams that would allow her to become a board-certified general surgeon—for so long, and now they were around the corner. Brian was right. These exams were what Zora needed to focus on. She'd overcome too many obstacles just to fail now, and she couldn't allow anything to distract her from this goal. All she needed was for everything in her life to go well from now until the exams were over.

Not that she expected to fail; Zora had done well enough on the yearly residency-in-training examinations to know she would excel in the boards. Yet she couldn't take anything for granted. She had nothing to lose by being extra prepared—scoring at the top of her class had helped her secure one of the coveted spots in her department's colorectal fellowship, a program she planned to enter once her residency was over.

Zora needed to make sure the spot remained hers without giving the hospital's and her department's leadership any reason to rescind her fellowship offer —she'd heard she hadn't been their favorite for the job, which wasn't surprising considering her history with the hospital.

Zora rubbed her forehead. "I know. Thanks for the reminder."

"And you need to find time to rest and do fun stuff, too. When was the last time you went on a date with Dave?" Dave was a lieutenant at the local police department, and Zora had reconnected with him when the organ trafficking case landed on her operating table.

They'd only started dating seriously six months ago, and everything had been great... until of late. As much as he'd tried to hide it, Zora could sense something had been bothering Dave. But he'd insisted it was only about the new case his team was working on. Still, the shadow of whatever it was had seeped into their time together, and Zora knew she had to convince Dave to get it off his chest soon. Being open in a relationship was important to her. She'd chosen to go out with him, flaws and all, and after all she'd been through, she couldn't imagine there was anything else that could shock her.

"I have a date with him this weekend," she replied. Maybe she could get Dave to open up then. Pretending everything was alright wasn't good enough for her. Something was wrong, and she needed to get to the bottom of it. "But I don't know."

Brian stared at Zora with concerned eyes. "What do you mean you don't know? Zora, is everything okay?"

Zora pinched the bridge of her nose. "I'm fine. We're fine. I'm sure it's nothing. Just the typical relationship stuff," she said.

Brian's phone buzzed at that moment, and he pulled it out from his pocket and glanced at the screen. His face brightened. There was only one person Zora knew that could put that look on his face. "I have to go," he said as he rose to his feet.

"Say hello to Christina for me."

Brian raised an eyebrow. "How did you know?"

"Is that even a question?" Christina was Zora's best friend and roommate, and she had been dating Brian for quite a while now.

Brian chuckled. "True." Then his face turned serious. "Zora, you'll let me know if anything is wrong, right?"

"I will. Now go before Christina calls again. You know we don't want that. I'll just stay and clean up this mess on the floor."

Brian nodded. "She hates waiting for sure. Alright, I'll see you later." He got up and left the room.

Zora leaned back. The call had been a lifesaver. The last thing she needed was Brian probing into her business. He was the sort that wouldn't let go until he uncovered the truth—something she was still working through herself.

Then she remembered something else that had been troubling her of recent. Zora had been living at the family home instead of her apartment since her sister, Alisa, came back into her life, so Dave had come by the house often. Alisa was cheerful and open with other friends and acquaintances of the family, but became the ice lady whenever Dave was around. Zora had asked her about it, but Alisa had deflected the question so smoothly Zora hadn't noticed she'd avoided it until much later.

Maybe it was time she had a sit-down with Alisa. Chatting with her may even shed some light on what was going on with Dave. Something told her the sooner she had the talk with Alisa, the better. Before it was too late.

But first, Zora had to clean up the mess on the floor and get through two days of night calls without any issues.

4

Alisa swept the sheets of paper off her rosewood desk to the floor, not caring as they scattered all over the plush grey carpet, intersecting the warm sun rays that streamed through the large floor-to-ceiling windows of her office. She grimaced and rubbed the back of her neck. Yet another useless report.

She'd started working in her mom's law firm—Smyth Law Associates, and one of the prominent law firms in Lexinbridge—as a senior legal associate in the corporate practice but with a corner office, unlike other associates at her level. Sure, it was nepotism, but her mom had all but proclaimed Alisa as her heir.

So Alisa worked extra hard to prove her mom had made the right decision, and soon it paid off. She'd brought in significant client revenue for the firm. The other associates had become more welcoming of her, and a few even stopped by for legal case advice. It seemed Alisa had inherited her mom's genius legal mind.

Yet she couldn't figure a way out of her current dilemma.

She slumped into the custom leather swivel chair, which matched the room's grey and rosewood decor, and let out a sigh. How was it the background checks were all the same? She'd hired investigator after investigator in the past few months to dig into Dave's background, but none had come up with anything else beyond what she'd gleaned about him from Zora.

Every report was clean, in fact, too pristine in her opinion. He was practically a boy scout—which only made her worry more. Sure, there were lots of folks like him who'd never committed a crime, but how was it possible he didn't even have one flaw?

She shifted in her seat. Alisa couldn't have been mistaken about who she'd seen on that fateful day. There was no way she could forget the face she'd glimpsed through the opened partition.

Alisa had dropped by the restaurant that fateful day after a long day at work. It was one of the many restaurants owned by her Russian mob family, and the beef stroganoff, made by the chef in the traditional way, was her father's favorite. She'd planned to surprise him with it. As Alisa had waited for the takeout, the partition to one of the private rooms opened, and one of her father's men stepped out.

It would have seemed normal, except this was one of Vaslav's henchmen. Which meant Vaslav—her father's right-hand man and a person she abhorred—was in that private room. Her father's men were terrible, but Vaslav was the worst of them all, with a deep, insatiable thirst for violence and bloodshed. If Vaslav was in there, he was up to no good. Besides, her father had rules about where they could hold meetings, and he considered this restaurant off-limits. What could Vaslav be up to? She had to find out.

Alisa angled herself until she had a line of sight to the entrance of the room and pretended to be reading some documents while she waited. She was sure Vaslav's man would be back soon—there was no way he'd leave Vaslav behind. A few minutes later, the man returned. As he opened the partition door to step in, Alisa glimpsed a striking, tall young man talking with Vaslav, who had a Russian cigar in his hand. From their somewhat relaxed postures, this was a man Vaslav was very familiar with, which meant the man wasn't someone she wanted to associate with. As the partition slid shut, the man glanced at the door, giving Alisa a full view of his face. Piercing brown eyes stared back at her unblinkingly.

Alisa froze for a moment, the features of his face committed to her memory. But it was the coldness of his eyes that warned her it was best for her to leave immediately. There was something fishy about what was going on in that room, and Alisa wanted no part of it.

Alisa feigned disinterest as the partition slid shut, though her heart thudded in her chest. Fortunately, the sous chef arrived with her order at that moment. Alisa accepted it and left the restaurant in haste. She'd told no one about the meeting and had eventually forgotten about it.

Until the day of the party when she'd seen those eyes again, in the features of the man she needed to boot as far away from her sister as possible. But how was she going to do that with no evidence? She hadn't wanted to reach out to any of the contacts she'd used before who could dig up even the color of the nightgown a subject's great-great-great grandmother used to wear to bed—the news would get back to her father, and she didn't want him involved in her life again.

Alisa had also wanted to avoid any investigators

that might have strong ties to the police—that would be like waving a red flag at Dave that she was looking into him. She ran her hands through her honey-colored hair. *Ugh*. What was she going to do now?

There was a brief knock on the door and Alisa looked up as it opened. A stunning, lithe brunette dressed in an impeccable dark-blue slim-fit suit, a crisp white shirt, and pump heels so high Alisa always wondered how she walked so well in them strode into the room and settled into a visitors' chair.

The brunette, Andrea Park, let out a loud sigh. "That was trying," she said, a smile flirting around the corners of her lips.

Alisa chuckled. Trust Andrea Park to be a little dramatic. She must have finished her scheduled meeting with an investment banking client, and Alisa was pretty sure some foolish VP or associate had tried to hit on her. They always did. Andrea must have put whoever it was in his place in her usual firm but sweet way.

Alisa had hit it off with Andrea as soon as she'd joined the firm, and they'd become so close Alisa had told her about her past—Andrea didn't seem to care. Andrea was also a senior associate in the corporate practice and had only been at the firm for over a year.

But rumors were already swirling that she would make partner soon. She was an ex-physician with a JD and an MBA, and her warm personality hid a keen mind. Andrea eschewed office politics, yet somehow got on well with most people at the firm. She was a wonderful ally to have. "I hope you didn't smack him too hard," Alisa said.

"No, no, no," Andrea responded as she shook her head. "You know I'm not a fan of violence. I only mistakenly stepped on his toes when his hand tried to brush my backside."

"Ouch!" The guy's toes must have been in a world of hurt if Andrea's stiletto-heeled shoes had gotten involved.

"That would teach him not to try it again. I expect he'll pay attention during his office's next sexual harassment training." Then Andrea seemed to notice the papers strewn all over the floor, and her face turned serious. "What's going on?"

Alisa leaned back. "I just need an excellent investigator."

"Then use the ones in the office."

"I'd rather not. It's a personal request."

"Hmmm. Have you reached out to Duncan Sawyer or Paula Verda? They're not tied to the firm, and they do good work."

"I've used them already. No dice."

"And I'm assuming someone from out-of-state won't work."

Alisa nodded. "I'd like to keep this close to home."

"Okay. Let me think some more about it. I'm sure we can come up with something." Andrea looked at the Rolex on her wrist. "Oh, it's already past lunchtime. Have you eaten?" Alisa shook her head. "How about that new café two streets away? I've only heard good things about it, and we can get some fresh air, too."

Well, sitting here and brooding about the dilemma would not solve Alisa's problem. Maybe getting some food in her would help. Besides, she had a long meeting in the afternoon, and she needed some fuel in her system before then. "Okay, let's go." She stood as Andrea also got to her feet.

Her phone rang, and Alisa glanced in its direction. Who could it be? She picked up the phone from where it rested on her desk and studied the screen. It was a number she didn't recognize, yet she swiped the answer button. "This is Alisa Smyth."

"Hello, Alisa," a familiar voice responded.

Alisa's breath caught. "Pete?" It was a voice from the dead. Pete had been her best friend for many years, until she'd learned her father had hired him and placed him by her side. He'd ended up tortured by her father for betraying his trust and helping Alisa. Alisa had negotiated with her father for his release, but Pete had disappeared soon after, and any attempts to find him had been futile. Knowing how resourceful Pete was, there was no need speculating about how he'd gotten her new number.

"Yes, it's me," he said.

"Oh my goodness! Where are you? Do you know how many times I've tried your number?"

Pete chuckled. "One question at a time. I'm in town. Would you like to meet up?"

"Sure. When would you like?"

"How about now?"

"Now?" She glanced at Andrea. Andrea gave her the okay sign. "Sure. But I have a meeting soon, so it won't be long."

"That's fine. How about that café with the swan statue two blocks away from your office?"

Alisa knew which coffee shop he was referring to. She'd been there a few times when she'd wanted to get away from the office. "You know where I work?"

"Isn't it public information?"

"Okay… you're right. I'll meet you there in about ten minutes."

"Alright. See you soon."

"Bye." Alisa ended the call. She was happy to hear from him, but why did Pete want to see her so urgently? There had to be a reason—one she couldn't think of now.

"Is this the Pete you told me about?" Andrea asked, her words invading Alisa's thoughts.

Alisa blinked and looked at Andrea. "Yes."

"I think you need to be careful," Andrea warned.

Alisa gave her a surprised look. "Why?"

"You've been trying to reach him for so long with no response. Then he calls you out of the blue and wants to meet? Something smells fishy."

Alisa twirled her phone in her hand. "Hmmm. Maybe, maybe not. But I won't know until I talk to him."

"Just be careful."

Alisa flashed her a smile. "Yes, I will. Why don't you go ahead so I don't hold you up?"

Andrea's eyes searched Alisa's. "Okay, but like I said, be careful."

"I will," Alisa reassured her. "Go. I'll see you later," she said.

Andrea nodded and left the office.

Alisa picked up the scattered papers on the floor and tucked them into a safe behind a hidden panel on the wall. Then she grabbed her phone and headed out.

She was looking forward to seeing Pete again

And maybe, just maybe, Pete might help her find a solution to her problem.

———

Alisa's eyes swept the space as she entered the quirky café, her shoulders relaxing as it always did anytime she entered this place. The café gave off a warm, inviting vibe, a place of respite for its customers from the fast-paced corporate life, with its watercolor paintings of swans gracing its white walls, swan-shaped seats in colors of black, white, or grey scattered around the room, and even salt and pepper shakers moulded into miniature swans. She loved coming here whenever she could.

The café was almost empty save for a few stragglers who remained after the shop's lunch hour. The smell of roast turkey and bacon greeted Alisa's nostrils, making her stomach rumble. She needed to get food into her stomach fast if she was going to survive the afternoon.

She spotted Pete seated at a table nestled into a

corner of the café and away from prying eyes. Instead of his signature immaculate attire, he was wearing a casual T-shirt that hung loosely on his frame and a pair of jeans. Yet he still looked as handsome as ever. He was so engrossed in whatever he was looking at on his phone that he didn't even notice Alisa's approach.

"Hello, Pete," she said.

Pete jumped like I'd caught him with his hand in a cookie jar. A frown creased his face as he looked up, then it morphed into a small smile as he noticed her. "Hey, Alisa." He got up and wrapped her in a hug. His familiar scent of aftershave washed over her, yet she could also smell scent tendrils of peppermint and cigarette smoke.

Alisa frowned. When had Pete started smoking? Was he under so much stress that he'd taken up the habit? Pete also looked thinner, but that was to be expected, considering what he'd gone through at the hands of Alisa's father. Well, her foster father, to be exact—his men had kidnapped her by mistake, and then he'd adopted her.

She released Pete and stared into his face. "How are you doing? Is your shoulder alright?" When Alisa had seen him last, he'd dislocated his left arm from the beating he'd received at her father's orders.

Pete moved around to pull out a chair for her.

"Thank you," Alisa said as she sat down.

Pete returned to his seat and settled in. "I'm okay," he said. "The shoulder got fixed." He demonstrated by rotating his arm. At her lingering gaze: "Really, I'm fine. Would you like anything?"

Alisa looked at the chalkboard on the wall behind the café's serving counter. "I'll have the clam chowder and sparkling water."

Pete pushed back his chair and stood up. "I'll be right back."

Alisa watched him head to the counter. There was something reserved about him, as though the experience he'd gone through at her father's hands had aged him. Or maybe that was just her imagination. He soon placed their order and then returned.

Alisa waited until he'd sat down and then asked, "Have you been in the country this whole time?"

His warm brown eyes stared back at her. "I'm sorry I avoided your calls. I needed some time to myself after what happened. And I'm sorry I worked for your father."

It had hurt when she'd found out. "Why did you?"

He picked up a salt shaker and twirled it in his

hands. "Remember how I told you a normal family was overrated?"

Alisa recalled the conversation. It was way before the truth about her parentage had come to light. "Yes, I do."

"My parents were supposed to be normal, or at least that's how everyone saw them. We lived in suburban America with all the expected trappings of a middle-income family. But they both began gambling, and everything went downhill from there. I came back from school one day to see men with guns sitting in the living room. It turned out my parents had lost everything at a high-stakes table and even owed a lot of money. So, they'd sold the only thing they had left. Me."

Alisa's eyes widened as shock rippled through her. "Are you kidding? How old were you?"

"Fifteen. I was told the only way I could leave was if I paid off their remaining debt. We're talking about hundreds of thousands of dollars. From what I saw of the men, there was no place I could run off to where they couldn't find me, and the consequences would have been disastrous. Your father discovered I was bright, so he allowed me to finish high school and then paid for my college education. I had to sign an agreement that I would work for him to pay the debt off. It turned out my first job was to keep you safe and ignorant."

"Ouch." Pete never did like to sugarcoat the truth.

"Sorry."

"What about your parents? Are they still alive?" Alisa asked.

Pete's lips tightened. "No idea, and I don't care to know."

A waiter arrived at that moment with their food. Pete had ordered a club sandwich and a glass of water for himself. The enticing smell of the chowder made Alisa want to dig in, but first she needed the answer to a question that had haunted her for months. "Were you ever really my friend?" she asked.

Pete's hand halted in mid-air, and he placed the glass of water he'd been holding back on the table. He met her gaze, his eyes laying the truth bare for her to see. "I had no friends when I met you, Alisa. So even though I was supposed to watch over you and report back, you were the first real friend I ever had. I didn't have to explain my background or anything with you."

"Do you still work for him? My father, I mean."

"No, he told me at the time he released me he never wanted to see me again." So her father had kept his promise.

"So, what do you want to do now?"

He stayed silent for a moment, as if mulling over what he was about to say. Then he looked into her eyes. "I'm going to travel for a while. Maybe even as far away as Africa."

So, he was going away. Far from her. Something told her it would never be the same between them. But no matter what had happened, Alisa would always miss him. "How long would you be gone?"

"Maybe a year, two years. I don't know. I think I need to figure out who I am again."

Alisa understood. She'd spent the past six months doing the same for herself. "I'll be here when you get back," she said softly. If he ever came back.

Pete's shoulders relaxed as if she'd rolled a boulder off his shoulders, like he'd been hoping to hear what she'd just said but hadn't dared to dream she'd actually say it. "But would your new family…?"

"I'm sure it'd be fine with them. My family isn't normal."

Pete laughed. "Alright." It was so nice to hear his laughter again. Their friendship might never be what it was before, but they could start anew and rebuild it bit by bit.

They dug into their meal in companionable silence.

The chowder was hot and delicious, and Alisa wished she could eat another bowl, but she was already full.

Soon it was time for Alisa to leave if she was to make her afternoon meeting. "When are you leaving?" she asked.

"This evening."

Her eyes widened. She hadn't expected it to be so soon. Even though her heart ached to hear it, there was nothing she could do but cheer him on. "Safe travels and try to stay in touch."

"I'll send you a text or email when I get there," he said.

"That would be great." Then she remembered what she'd wanted to ask him. "Pete, I need a discreet private investigator. Someone who doesn't have deep connections with the local PD."

Pete's eyes assessed her. "I'm assuming you don't want to use any of our old guys."

"Yes."

He thought for a moment. "There's a guy an acquaintance reminded me of a few days ago. A man called Charles, who helped him resolve a hard case that had troubled him. This Charles is relatively new compared to the others we've worked with, but I've heard he gets the job done."

Alisa's heart perked up at the news. "Do you have his number?"

Pete nodded. "I thought what he did was impressive, so I took his number down just in case. I'll text it to you." He pulled out his phone and punched in some keys. "I haven't used him before, and I'd still tread carefully, regardless."

"Why?"

"I've heard he doesn't enjoy meeting his clients in person. He takes care of everything over the phone and email. That's odd. I'm wary of guys who don't do things the regular way."

Oh, that was different. But maybe the guy wasn't a people person. "Do you know why?"

Pete shook his head. "No idea. I wondered if he had something to hide, but the people who've used him seemed satisfied."

Alisa's phone beeped. She looked at the screen and noticed a text message had come in. It was Charles' number. "Thanks."

"No problem. Like I said, just be careful with him."

"I will. I have to go." Alisa stood up.

Pete got to his feet as well. "Take care of yourself, Alisa."

She reached out and pulled him into a hug. "You too. And lose the cigarettes, will you?"

Pete chuckled. "Yes, ma'am," he said as she released him.

Alisa gave him one last look, turned, and left the café. She wasn't sure if she'd ever see him again, but she was glad they'd reconnected one more time.

But now she had a number to call.

Maybe she'd make some headway at last and get the answers she needed about Dave.

Alisa shut the door of her office behind her and closed the shades lining the floor-to-ceiling windows that looked out into the bullpen where most junior associates worked. She needed all the privacy she could get for the call she was about to make.

She pulled out the burner phone she kept for times like this and dialed the number Pete had given her.

"Hello," a raspy voice intoned.

"Hi, I'd like to speak with Charles, the private investigator," Alisa said.

"This is he."

"I'd like to discuss a job with you."

"My office is on the second floor of 40 Crescent Street, Suite 212. When would you like to drop by?"

Alisa's brow furrowed. This was strange. Hadn't Pete said the guy was strictly an email or phone communicator? "I've heard you don't meet clients in person."

"That was before I got an office of my own," he replied. "Never liked public places either."

His answer satisfied Alisa somewhat, though a part of her remembered Pete's warning. She'd heard of people like this. Besides, Crescent Street was in a safe commercial area of downtown Lexinbridge. The neighborhood had gone downhill over time with some businesses shuttering, but the city was looking to revive the area, and now it had lots of ongoing construction work and new businesses opening there.

"So when will you be coming by?" His question cut through Alisa's thoughts and brought her back to the present.

"How about today at four-thirty p.m.?" That was about an hour away. It would give her enough time to wrap up her work here and yet be early enough to get in and out of Crescent Street before dark. Alisa could defend herself if needed with all her extensive martial arts training, but it was best to exercise caution.

"Sure, I'll be here," he responded.

"Alright. See you then." She ended the call.

———————————

An hour later, Alisa sat in one of two Victorian chairs —the type she might have seen at Aunt Matilda's house—that seemed at odds with the rest of the sparsely furnished cream-walled room. The building hadn't been difficult to find, and Charles' office was at the end of the long hallway. She'd almost expected to see a man wearing a cravat and a top hat, but Charles was a bespectacled man in his early forties, dressed in an unassuming sports jacket over a white button-down shirt. He looked more like a professor than anything else.

"Nice to meet you, Miss…"

"Alisa."

"Okay. How may I help you, Miss Alisa?"

He was direct, ready to get down to business. "I'd like a thorough background check on a man. Is that something you can do?"

"That shouldn't be a problem."

"I need this to be quiet."

"It's what I'm good at. What's the name?"

"Dave McKesson." Alisa watched closely, but

there was no change in Charles' demeanor at the mention of the name. *Good*.

"Any other information about him?" Charles asked.

"He works with the local PD."

Charles raised an eyebrow. "You're investigating a cop?"

"That's why I need it to be quiet. It can't get back to him."

"I'll take care of it. Discretion is my watchword."

"When will the report be ready?" Alisa asked.

"In a week." A week was fine, though Alisa would have preferred getting it faster. "I have to go out of town for the next few days for another client's work," he clarified.

"Okay." She'd waited months. She could do another week.

"I'll get back to you once it's ready," Charles said. "I'm assuming the number you called me from is the best way to reach you."

"Yes. How much will this cost?"

He shook his head. "No need for it yet. I prefer payment after the report is ready. Don't worry, my rates are reasonable." This was unconventional—most investigators preferred a down payment, if anything, but it wasn't enough to raise any red flags.

"Alright." Alisa stood to her feet. "I'll wait to hear from you."

He rose as well and extended his hand for a shake. "See you soon, Miss Alisa."

Alisa shook his hand. It was cold and clammy, not what she'd expected, and she dropped it quickly. Time to head out.

She turned and made for the exit. As she stepped over the threshold, her foot slipped and Alisa landed on the floor, the contents of her small purse spilling all over.

Ouch. Her butt hurt from its hard contact with the floor, and she could feel a throbbing pain in her ankle. She looked around for the offending cause of her fall and saw a fresh banana peel beyond the threshold.

Hold on! This hadn't been here on my way in, she thought. Or had it? No, she was pretty sure it wasn't there before.

Her anger rose at whoever had dropped it. How hard would it have been to discard the banana peel in a trash can instead of the floor? Alisa doubted any office on this level didn't have one. She gathered her items back into her purse.

"Are you alright?" Charles had made it to her side. *He moves fast,* she thought. He noticed the banana peel, and his mouth curled in disgust. "I'm sorry about that." A faint scent of disinfectant washed over her now that he'd come so close.

Alisa's senses prickled even as her ankle throbbed. What could Charles be doing with disinfectant in this office? That was when she noticed the few things in the space seemed to be positioned just so, nothing out of order, the tiled floor spotless. *He's probably OCD and maybe a germaphobe*, she thought. She tried to get up, but a sharp pain jolted through her ankle, forcing her to remain on the floor.

"Let me help you," Charles said. He handed over her remaining items and then lifted Alisa to her feet like she weighed nothing, like he was a man who was no stranger to weights and she was just another dumbbell. "How's your ankle now?"

Alisa tested it. It still hurt, but it seemed like it was only a sprain and nothing worse. If she treaded carefully, she could make it to the building's entrance with no issues. "It's okay. Thanks."

"I can help you down to your car."

"It's fine." She tried a step and then another. It hurt a little, but nothing she couldn't bear. Alisa was pretty sure all she needed was an ice pack, pain killers, leg elevation, and some rest, to make her ankle as good as new.

"Alright. Take care, Miss Alisa," Charles said.

"Thank you." Alisa could feel his eyes on her back as she made her way down the hallway to the elevators. She hadn't planned for an ankle sprain, but the trip had been worth it.

Now she could get the evidence she needed.

5

"Dr. Smyth, could please look at the leg trauma patient? I believe his mental state has deteriorated since he was last seen."

Zora looked up from the computer terminal she'd been typing into. She was a couple hours into her second-day call, and so far it had been relatively quiet compared to how it was on a typical Friday night. "Isn't that Herbert's patient?" she asked the nurse who stood in front of her.

The nurse nodded. "We've paged him multiple times, but we can't reach him. We also paged the attending, Dr. Bennett, but he just called back to say he's stuck in traffic on George Hamilton and asked that you check the patient on his behalf." The city had just started some reconstruction work on the bridge from evenings until dawn, so bottlenecked traffic on it was pretty common.

Not Herbert again! Zora thought. It seemed he hadn't learned his lesson, even after a patient had died on his watch yesterday. Why did she have to be on call with him yet again today?

Zora logged off and strode toward the patient's cubicle with the nurse in tow. She soon reached it and entered. Her third-year resident, Dr. Evan Johnson, was already examining the patient lying on the gurney. "I overheard the call from Dr. Bennett and figured I'd get a head-start on him," he said.

"So, what do we have here?" Zora pulled a pair of gloves from the dispenser on the wall, donned them, and began a physical and neurological examination of the patient, who appeared disoriented.

"James Connor, a twenty-nine-year-old grad student, fell down the stairs of his apartment and arrived conscious and alert to the ER with trauma to the left lower limb," Dr. Johnson said. "CT scan of the left lower limb showed no bone or soft tissue damage except for a skin laceration on the left calf. Patient received a couple stitches to the calf and is under observation for a few hours to be discharged later tonight."

"Any history of head trauma?"

"None noted on his initial assessment, and his friend who brought him in doesn't know."

Zora halted her examination. She could feel her blood beginning to boil. A patient had fallen down the stairs, and the first doctor who'd seen him hadn't bothered to check for possible head trauma? Even medical students knew to ask. This was a lawsuit waiting to happen! She took a deep breath to calm herself. "Any drug or alcohol history, family history of epilepsy, or any platelet disorders?"

"None that we know of," Dr. Johnson responded.

"Any headaches or vomiting since he arrived?" she asked the nurse.

The nurse shook her head. "None."

Zora turned back to the patient, and the room's other occupants stayed silent as she completed her examination. There was no obvious skull fracture, spinal injury, or extremity weakness. Patient had a Glasgow Coma Scale score of twelve, but the cognitive and motor balance functions were difficult to test. "Nurse, could we elevate his head and get some oxygen on him?" The nurse moved to comply.

Zora turned back to her resident. "Let's send a consult to Neurosurgery to come and see this patient. In the meantime, let's get a head CT done and order a full blood workup, including glucose and electrolyte panels, blood alcohol level, and a toxicology screen. Page me once we have the results."

"The neurosurgery resident is already in the ER seeing another patient," the nurse offered.

"Perfect," Zora replied. "Thank you."

"On it," Dr. Johnson responded and hurried out of the cubicle.

Zora stripped off her gloves and dumped them in the secure waste bin. "Let's monitor him closely," she said to the nurse. "And let me know if anything changes before Neuro takes over his case."

"We'll take care of him," the nurse promised.

"Thank you," Zora said as she squirted some sanitizer into her hands from its dispenser and rubbed them together. Then she left the cubicle.

She rotated one shoulder, then another, to relieve the ache in them as she walked through the ER and back to the computer terminal she'd been using. Zora was tired and exhausted and still had some board exam reviews to finish tonight in between attending to patients. Now there was one more reason to complete her residency successfully and do well at the boards: she would never have to work with Herbert again, even if the department did nothing about him—he considered the colorectal fellowship too *boring*.

But first, she needed to get through tonight.

Zora prayed the rest of the call would be uneventful.

Noxious gas filled Zora's nostrils, cutting off her oxygen supply. She choked and grabbed her throat, reaching for the door, but it refused to budge. Her eyes darted around the room for anything she could use to cover her nose and mouth, but everything her hands grabbed seemed soldered to the nearest surface. Zora's eyes watered, making it hard to see, yet she kept searching. This was not the way she'd planned to die.

Someone banged on the other side of the floor-to-ceiling glass that enclosed one side of the wall, and Zora looked up. The unknown guy lifted a chair and rammed it against the glass, but it refused to give way. Zora could feel his terror, and it wrapped around her heart, squeezing it hard.

No! There has to be a way. She couldn't give up like this. After being kidnapped, stabbed in jail, and almost dying in the hands of a serial killer, how could she die here, stuck in what looked like a lab?

But her body weakened, and Zora fell to her knees. She tried to hold her breath and not inhale, but soon she felt rings of darkness shadowing her vision as her body turned to jelly and she collapsed flat on the floor. Tears escaped from the corners of her eyes and regret filled her as she watched her life and her dreams fading away…

Zora jerked awake and sat up. She struggled to fill her lungs with air like a man who'd starved of air for a long time. Her eyes darted around the room until she recognized where she was… The residents' on-call room. Her heart pounded in her chest as she brushed sweat-soaked strands of hair away from her face. Then she repeated Psalm Twenty-Three until her heart rate calmed.

Thank goodness no one else was in the room. It'd been a while since she'd had any nightmares, and this time she remembered the details as vividly as the first surgery she'd ever done. Unfortunately, she didn't recognize the location of the lab and the man that had been fighting to save her life.

Zora got up and walked over to the window to clear her head. Dawn was already beginning to break, which meant Zora's call would be over soon.

She stared out at the sky with its soft blue glow and fluffy white clouds that sung of warm summer days to come. Small birds flitted from one branch to the next on trees that had shed their memories of winter and its somber stark majesty. Instead, they were now dotted with buds ready to open into the light, the promise of spring blossom and new leaves to come. The early morning sun broke through with cloud-filtered rays washing over the back gardens as they threw off their subdued colors in favor of blooming flowers and lush greens. The view looked so peaceful and innocent, a deep contrast to the nightmare she'd just experienced.

But she couldn't afford to dwell on the dream she'd had. Her call wasn't over, and she still had patients to see. Zora needed to pull herself together.

She turned away from the window with a sigh, headed into the attached bathroom, and splashed water on her face. Zora cleaned herself up as quickly as she could and soon returned to where she'd been studying before she'd dozed off.

But she couldn't stop thinking about the dream. What had it meant? Zora had had nightmares after her sister went missing—it usually heralded some bad event. But now her sister was back in her life. Was the nightmare still a warning that something terrible was about to happen? Zora hoped not—she'd had enough misfortune to last a lifetime.

Her pager beeped. Zora unsnapped it from its hook on the waistband of her scrubs and scanned the message on it. There was another patient waiting for her care. Duty called, and she had to take care of it ASAP.

But Zora hoped everything would be smooth sailing from now on until the board exams.

Because she wasn't sure if she could survive any more upheavals in her life.

Lucas leaned back against the chicken wire that encircled the exercise area. His boys surrounded him, their howling wolf tattoos peeking out from the side of their necks, and the smell of unwashed bodies pervading the air. From the corner of his eye, he could see the prison guards monitoring the area.

Other prisoners in the space had enough sense to stay away or avoid looking in their direction, unless they wanted to bleed out in the communal shower room, watching helplessly as their blood drained down the rusty shower drain. Lucas remained as alert as ever, even though he feigned disinterest in what was going on around him—a rival prison gang member could summon up courage and attack at anytime.

He hadn't heard from the man. Sure, it was too soon, but the man had built a reputation for surprising clients and doing whatsoever he wanted. No one cared as long as he delivered the goods on time. So Lucas hoped he'd hear from him soon.

He had to destroy Dave McKesson. Lucas' blood boiled at the mere thought of his name. Dave had taken away something precious to Lucas that could never be replaced. Horrifying images of how he'd lost the beautiful gift invaded his mind at night, leaving him tortured and worn out in the morning. There was no way he could continue suffering through this alone—Dave had to join him in this hell.

A hand grabbed his from the other side of the barbed wire. Lucas' skin prickled, and his first instinct was to thrust the shiv hidden in his waistband into the hand behind him and destroy the nerves that enabled it to grip him. But something warned him that would be a terrible idea.

He waited, his body on high alert, to see what the hand would do.

A piece of green-colored paper slipped into Lucas' palm, and then the hand withdrew.

Lucas' heart raced. He pretended to cough and

then swallowed the paper instead. He knew without looking that there was nothing written on it.

But it was a message.

The hunt was on. Now all Lucas had to do was wait for the good news.

He looked up at the sun bright in the sky despite the cool air, and he smiled.

Yes, today was a good day.

7

"Tell me about this patient," Zora said to Dr. Johnson, who was already in the cubicle when Zora arrived. The patient, a white male, appeared to be in his late twenties and seemed semi-conscious, but in pain. They'd set up the IV line, and it now snaked its way into his forearm.

"Oliver Young, a twenty-eight-year-old male, presented to the ER with a stab wound to the left lumbar region by an unknown assailant," Dr. Johnson said. "Patient appears semi-conscious, but responsive to pain, with a Glasgow Coma Scale score of thirteen. Lungs are clear and well perfused, BP is hundred over sixty, heart is in sinus rhythm, but there is tenderness in the left lumbar region with reduced bowel sounds. Paracentesis of the abdomen yielded some blood.

"CT scan shows possible internal bleeding, but the kidney and spleen appear normal." Dr. Johnson handed over the CT scan, which Zora examined.

"What about the blood work?" Zora asked.

"Appears normal except for a mild neutrophil count increase, but hemoglobin, total WBC, lymphocytes, eosinophils, monocytes, and basophils are within the normal range."

Zora accepted the tablet from Dr. Johnson and scanned the lab results. The numbers were like he'd said. The normal hemoglobin level didn't preclude internal bleeding, and maybe the neutrophil count indicated that infection was just beginning to set in. "Any history of allergies?"

"None," Dr. Johnson replied. "I asked his mother. She came with him in the ambulance."

"Have we notified the cops?" Zora asked as she grabbed a set of gloves and donned them. The state law required any gunshot or stab wound to be reported to the police.

"Yes," Dr. Johnson replied. "And we've taken pictures of the wound."

"Good." Zora bent and examined the abdomen. It appeared distended with reduced bowel sounds. The wound was warm to touch and looked like a serrated knife had carved it, though the cops would better identify the specific weapon used.

"We took a swab of the wound and sent it to the lab," Dr. Johnson said. "We expect the STAT results to be out soon."

"Okay, let's get him to the OR. And make sure we have cross-matched blood on standby, just in case."

Dr. Johnson hesitated. "Shouldn't we stabilize him and then hand him over to the next team? Our call should be over in about ten minutes."

Zora glanced sharply at Dr. Johnson. She could see the dark circles under his eyes, and how his body sagged with exhaustion. Still… "A lot can happen in ten minutes," Zora rebuked him in a quiet voice. "It's our job to take care of each patient to the best of our abilities."

Some people might have said surgeons must feel like gods having the power of life and death over patients, but they didn't understand how heavy the responsibility was. Surgeons had to push through and make rational decisions for each patient, no matter how tired or exhausted they were, even if it meant putting their own lives at stake. They could be hit with a malpractice lawsuit even after providing the best of care, still they had to do everything they could to save the patient's life. It was important that Dr. Johnson understood that.

Zora patted his shoulder. "I know you're tired, but we need to do all we can for this patient," she said. "Besides, I think he might be in a lot more pain than he's letting on. Let's get him to the OR."

Zora stepped into the OR, the air chilly as usual. She noticed the operating table, which was the central focus of the large white-walled room, was empty.

She looked around. Where was the patient? She'd expected the gurney to be here by now. Zora had taken a detour to the on-call room to change her scrubs after explaining the risks of the surgery in detail to the patient's family, and had then called the attending about the case, so she'd expected the patient to have arrived in the OR. But the only persons present in the room were the on-call anesthe-siologist waiting for the patient, the peri-operative nurse and the surgical tech, who were prepping the sterile area and sorting the surgical instruments, and the circulating nurse, who was observing the room's activities.

An uneasiness flickered through Zora. This

wasn't good. Maybe she was being paranoid after the nightmare, but she didn't like when things didn't run like they were supposed to.

She turned to the peri-operative nurse, someone she'd worked with in multiple surgical cases. "Hello, Nurse Weaver. Has the patient been here?" Zora asked. But Nurse Weaver didn't get a chance to respond.

"Incoming!" a voice said from behind her.

Zora turned to see the surgical orderlies wheeling the patient into the OR.

Thank goodness. Then her forehead furrowed. But where was Dr. Johnson, who was supposed to have been with the patient during transportation? As if reading her mind, Dr. Johnson stepped into the OR, all scrubbed and ready to go.

Zora beckoned him over to the side while the OR staff prepped the patient. "What happened?" she asked.

"We had a bit of delay," he said. "There was some shift handover that took place with the orderlies right after you left, and the cops stopped by to see the patient while we waited for the handover to end. Then the surgical elevator got stuck, so we waited for that too."

"We're ready for you," Dr. Meyer, the anesthesiologist, called out.

The patient was here now, and time was ticking away.

Zora headed to the patient's side, and 'time out' began. Zora and the surgical team confirmed the patient, side and site of surgery, the procedure to be performed, patient's position, and the surgical instruments needed for the operation. They also reviewed the relevant radiological images. The outcome was pretty routine in this case, and everything was as expected. Then Zora donned the operating gown and gloves with the help of the surgical tech, confirmed the starting time, bent her head for a quick prayer, and then began the surgery. "Scalpel."

The peri-operative nurse handed it to her, and the surgery was underway. Soon, Zora had cut through the peritoneum and inserted the retractors. Dr. Johnson applied the suction catheter, and bright red blood gurgled into a glass reservoir. Zora then pressed in laparotomy pads to absorb any excess blood, making it easier to hunt down the bleeder.

She started searching for it with the spleen. Zora examined its surface and soon found a laceration on its anterior side.

Her chest tightened, and she frowned. This was

strange. "Can we put up the patient's CT scan?" she asked. The circulating nurse brought the scan to her side. Zora studied it. Yes, it was as she'd imagined. The splenic surface appeared intact on the film. So why was there a major laceration on the actual spleen? "Dr. Johnson, what do you think about the spleen on this CT?"

"Normal."

"How about this spleen?" Zora gestured to the one in her hand.

"That's odd," Dr. Johnson said. "A laceration of this size, including some subcapsular or parenchymal hematomas from it, should have been apparent on the CT scan."

"Exactly."

"BP is dropping!" Dr. Meyer called out. He hung up a bag of fresh blood and increased its flow. Thank goodness Zora had requested extra blood.

The mystery of the splenic laceration had to be shelved for the time being. It was more important to save the patient first and then figure it out later. "Three-oh prolene," Zora called out.

The peri-operative nurse handed it over, and Zora sutured the lacerated edges of the spleen together, then applied fibrin glue. The splenic bleeding stopped. "How are we doing?" she asked Dr. Meyer.

"BP is back at ninety-eight over sixty. Sinus tach," he responded.

Zora's shoulders relaxed. This was good. She removed the previous laparotomy pads and packed in another set. Then she checked the kidney and other adjoining organs. There were no additional lacerations. Good. Now they were on the home stretch.

Suddenly, a blare from the monitor pierced the air.

"BP is crashing again! Systolic at seventy-five," Dr. Meyer called out.

Zora removed the new laparotomy pads she'd just inserted. There was hardly any blood on them. So what was causing the BP to drop?

"Crap," Dr. Meyer muttered.

Zora's eyes jerked to him. "What's going on?"

"It's anaphylactic shock," he replied.

Zora's heart dropped. Anaphylactic shock was one of a surgeon's worst nightmares, was life-threatening and had to be resolved quickly, or it could lead to death.

"Patient now has red wheals all over his skin," the circulating nurse stated. At this announcement, the peri-operative nurse moved to support the anesthesiologist. He was going to need all the help he could get.

It was anaphylactic shock if the patient now had urticaria. Zora rejected the fear that threatened to coil up in her stomach. Thank goodness the hospital now used synthetic gloves in the OR, ruling out a possible latex allergy. She, no, they could do this. They could save the life of this patient. "Let's get one milligram of epinephrine IV going in."

"Already in," Dr. Meyer responded. "NMBA discontinued. Oxygen at a hundred percent. Two liters of saline going in at maximum flow rate with IV crystalloid, with more fluid to follow." NMBAs were neuromuscular blocking agents used to facilitate intubation, decrease patient movement, and improve muscle relaxation for abdominal surgery, but they had the very rare risk of causing anaphylaxis in a few patients. Giving the crystalloid as well compensated for the peripheral vasodilation that often accompanied anaphylaxis.

Zora turned to the circulating nurse. "Let's place the patient in the Trendelenburg position." This elevation of the patient's legs would help blood flow to the brain and heart. Once that was done: "Could you also get the attending on the line and get the crash cart in here?" she asked.

"Sure." The circulating nurse hurried off to take care of it.

Then Zora turned to the resident. "Since there are no other bleeders, let's close up this patient. Can you handle that?"

"Yes," he responded and got on it ASAP.

"How's the pulse? Heart rhythm?" Zora asked Dr. Meyer.

"Weak with tachycardia, but still in sinus rhythm."

"Airway?"

"There is some angioedema and bronchospasm going on, but the intubation is getting the oxygen into his lungs. Patient is now on albuterol nebulizer and we've given him five mg per kg hydrocortisone IV and diphenhydramine." Angioedema of the pharynx, larynx and trachea caused upper airway obstruction, whereas bronchospasm resulted in lower airway obstruction. The albuterol would help with bronchodilation, while the hydrocortisone would decrease airway swelling and prevent recurrence of symptoms. There was still hope. Maybe they could turn this around soon.

The circulatory nurse returned and pressed a phone close to Zora's ear. "Dr. Bennett," Zora said.

"What's going on, Dr. Smyth?" Dr. Bennett asked.

"Stab wound patient in anaphylactic shock.

Possible allergic reaction to NMBA. We have hypotension, tachycardia, angioedema, and possible bronchospasm. One mg of epinephrine IV given. Patient is now on hundred percent oxygen, two liters of normal saline going in at the fastest rate, has received hydrocortisone, and is on nebulized albuterol."

"Let's give another dose of epinephrine. I'm on my way."

"Sounds good." Zora indicated to the circulating nurse that she was done. "Thank you," she said. The nurse left to return the phone. "How is the BP now?" she asked Dr. Meyer.

"Still dropping."

Zora's heart rate increased, though her demeanor didn't change. This could turn into a grade IV anaphylactic shock with cardiovascular collapse, a situation they needed to prevent. "Let's give another dose of epinephrine. If the hypotension persists, we may need to set up an epinephrine infusion."

"Done."

The circulating nurse returned, pushing in the crash cart and placing it in position for easy access.

"How are we doing with the closure?" Zora asked Dr. Johnson.

"Just finished."

"Good."

"He's in V-fib!" Dr. Meyer called out.

The tension in the room rose and was palpable enough to cut with a knife. What Zora had feared had come true. Yet they had to keep fighting to save the patient.

"Start CPR," she said. Johnson started compressing the patient's chest.

Zora glanced at the monitor. The rhythm looked chaotic. "Paddles ready? One-twenty joules."

The circulating nurse placed the defibrillator paddles on the patient's chest. "Everyone, step back!" she yelled.

The paddles discharged, and the patient's torso jerked.

Johnson resumed the chest compressions. "Still in V-fib!" Dr. Meyer said after a minute.

"Another milligram of epinephrine IV, and then we'll shock again at one-twenty," Zora ordered.

Dr. Meyer gave the epinephrine. Then it was time for another shock of the paddles, and the patient jerked at the impact. The surgical tech took notes.

The attending arrived, and Zora updated him on the current status.

"Let's give Amiodarone 300 milligrams IV," the

attending ordered as he examined the patient. The drug made its way into the patient through the line.

All eyes were glued to the monitor as the tension escalated. But the V-fib was relentless even as CPR continued like clockwork.

Then the rhythm flatlined. "Asystole!" Dr. Meyer called out.

"Another milligram of epinephrine IV," the attending responded.

Dr. Meyer administered the dose, but the flatline refused to budge.

The tension filled the room like a fog.

CPR continued for the next thirty minutes with all efforts made to maintain the patient's circulation, airway, and breathing. They checked the rhythm and pulse every two minutes and administered epinephrine every four minutes, yet there was no change.

But Zora and the team refused to give up and administered CPR for another thirty minutes.

Then the attending turned to everyone. "Stop CPR," he said. He listened to the patient's chest and checked the pupillary response, central pulse, and motor reaction to pain. He moved over to the cardiac monitor—an asystolic pattern dominated the screen, and the doppler showed no cardiac motion or blood flow.

Finally, he looked around at everyone in the OR. "I believe additional heroic measures are futile, and I'm ready to call the code. Are we all in agreement?"

Everyone in the OR, including Zora, echoed their assent. It was time.

"Okay," he said. "Time of death is six-thirty p.m."

And even though Zora had been expecting it, her heart sank with the pronouncement.

She'd just had her first table death—a death on her operating table.

Her nightmare had begun.

8

All hell broke loose from that point on. The hospital sent out notification alerts about the death to the hospital risk management committee and informed the county's coroner's office, with everything related to the patient's death now under his jurisdiction. They also alerted the cops, since it was a stab wound case.

At a family conference with Dr. Meyer, Nurse Weaver, a chaplain, and a social worker present, Zora broke the news of the patient's death to the family. The attending stayed by her side and answered their questions, for which Zora was grateful.

"Are you alright?" Dr. Bennett asked as they made their way down the corridor, the sobs from the patient's mother echoing through the doors of the conference room they'd just exited.

Zora nodded, even though her heart ached and her legs felt as heavy as lead as she walked beside him. "I'm fine," she said.

"It's always hard," he said sympathetically. "This is your first table death, right?"

"Yes," she responded, swallowing the lump in her throat.

Dr. Bennett halted, and Zora stopped as well. "You did all you could to save the patient," he said as he placed a reassuring hand on her shoulder. "It's not your fault, okay?"

Zora gave him a small smile. "Okay."

"Good." He dropped his hand and resumed walking. Zora matched his steps. "This may not be a good time to mention this, but you need to know they've included this case in Monday's Morbidity & Mortality conference. It's standard protocol, as you know."

"But aren't we going to need the autopsy results for it? Today is Saturday."

"The coroner's office has granted permission for the autopsy to be done at our morgue. So I called in a favor, and the pathologists have agreed to have a preliminary report ready for us in time for the meeting."

"Thank you."

"You're welcome. Since you have the rest of the weekend off, take some time to rest and then come back refreshed on Monday. Don't be afraid to seek a grief counselor if you need one. We've all been through this one time or the other, and there's nothing shameful about doing so. Sound good?"

"Yes."

"Alright. See you later, Dr. Smyth."

Zora watched as the attending strode in the stairwell's direction. She was too tired to do the same, so she headed instead to the set of elevators and took one down to the next floor. Even though her call was over, she needed to finish her notes for the case and then pick up her things from her locker before heading out.

She entered the residents' on-call room. The room, which had been buzzing right before she'd set foot in it, grew quiet. Zora ignored everyone and headed to the workstation in a corner of the lounge.

"I heard you killed a patient," Herbert's harsh voice stated.

His words shook her to the core. This was a terrible thing for anyone to say to her and the last thing she needed. She'd thought about stopping by a boxing gym and working out her frustration on a heavy bag, but maybe a long-overdue showdown with Herbert might take the edge off first.

Zora steeled herself and turned in his direction. The other residents held their breath as if unsure of what was going to happen, yet were keen to see it. "At least I did everything to save my patient," she said. "You killed your patient with your stupidity."

Zora heard the collective sharp inhales at her words. Herbert's nostrils flared, and his eyes bulged. He took a couple of steps toward her. "What did you say?"

Zora cocked her head. "Do we need to check your ears, too?"

Herbert charged toward her. "How dare you—"

"Easy there, big fellow." Ian, one of the other chief residents, stood in his way. "You guys can't do this here."

Zora ignored them both and soon reached the workstation and settled in. She heard the door slam hard and guessed Herbert had left the room.

"Zora—"

Zora turned to the voice that had called her name. "I don't need a lecture now, Ian. It's been a long day."

"I'm sorry about what happened," Ian said.

Zora's expression softened. "Thanks."

"If it's any consolation, the mortality review of both your cases will be on Monday."

Interesting. So Herbert was going to face the music at last, though Zora could bet he'd find a way to wriggle out of it. She gave Ian a small smile. "Thanks for telling me."

"I'll leave you to it."

Zora turned back to the workstation, signed in, and spent the next thirty minutes updating her notes for the case. Soon she was done, and she logged out of the system.

She looked around the room. The other residents might have sensed she needed her space, because they'd all left.

Zora sighed and leaned back. No one had told her a death on the operating table could be this draining. She was emotionally spent from grieving the loss of the patient. Even though she knew it wasn't her fault, the patient had died on her watch. All her mind wanted to do was replay the event to see if there was anything she'd missed. Yet she couldn't continue this way. She'd never be able to help other patients if she allowed the death to consume her.

But her mind refused to budge from the case. Why had the patient died despite all the immediate emergency treatment they'd given him? Yes, it happened sometimes, but the patient's medical history indicated this was the first time he'd received NMBAs, since he'd had no prior surgery or intubation. So why had his reaction been so severe? She couldn't wait to see what the autopsy results would say.

Zora rubbed the back of her neck. The nightmare had truly been a sign, with what just happened. But was this the end of it? There had been a man in her dream who'd tried to save her, and that hadn't matched with today's events. Did that mean more was coming?

God, help me. She couldn't deal with more. Right now, she couldn't even focus on her board exam review after what had happened. Could she imagine how terrible it would be if more catastrophe took place?

Zora pulled off her hair tie and ran her hands through her hair. *Aargh.* Why couldn't she just have a peaceful life like everyone else? It wasn't like she sought these situations. Folks might say a peaceful life was vanilla, but she craved the taste just the same. Instead, Zora had to deal with the M & M conference and whatever else that came her way because of the patient's death.

She let her head fall forward. She'd planned to rest at her family home after the call, and then chat with her sister about Dave later that night. But that couldn't happen now. There was no way she was going home to them. Her mother and sister had only to look at her face, and they would ferret out the truth of what happened today from her, something she wasn't ready to talk about with them.

Zora rose to her feet and walked over to her locker. A part of her wanted to call Dave and tell him what happened, but the other half just wanted to have a pity party alone. Her news could also distract him when he needed all his focus on this case he couldn't talk about. Maybe she'd wait until the dinner date and tell him then.

But for now, there was only one place she wanted to be.

Zora changed out of her scrubs, grabbed her things, and headed out.

9

Dave McKesson strode down the hallway that led to the captain's office. It had been a few months since they'd promoted him to lieutenant, and he was enjoying the role, even though he missed being on the ground as much as he had in the past. But the biggest benefit was he now had more time to date Zora, who'd become the most important person in his life.

He'd never thought they'd be together again after Zora had pushed him and her other friends away when her sister had gone missing. Only Christina had remained by her side.

But he was glad she hadn't been in his life during the years he'd been an undercover detective for the New York Police Department—he would have brought danger to her door. Dave had dealt with devils and monsters, and at some point, he'd become one to fit in and maintain his cover. By the time he'd risen to the surface for air, his mind had been so damaged by the real-life nightmares he'd witnessed that he'd begged for a transfer to his hometown, Lexinbridge. Even though devils existed in this town, and he'd made a trip or two here while he'd been undercover, he didn't have to pretend to be one of them. He'd relearned to live, and then he'd met Zora.

It had surprised Dave when Zora had shown interest in rekindling their relationship, since he felt he didn't deserve her. She was clean and bright and all things hopeful, while he was darkness and despair. Yet she'd dug in and brought out—no, demanded—the boy he'd been once before.

Spending time with Zora had encouraged Dave to rediscover himself, and now he dreamed again of family and love and all the other good things in this world. It'd scared him when he'd almost lost her to the jail system, and even more so when the cartel had kidnapped her, making Dave determined to keep her safe no matter what it took. He loved everything about her and appreciated all her friends and family who'd welcomed him into their lives. Well, except for her sister, Alisa.

Dave wasn't certain what the issue was, but it was plain to see that she disliked him. When she stared at him, it was as if she could glimpse his darkness, the rotten parts of him he hadn't been able to excise, yet she'd never said anything or confronted him. But how could she tell? It wasn't like he'd done anything to her to earn her hostility. Yet he hoped he'd be able to win her over some day.

He soon reached the captain's office and knocked on the door.

"Come in," a gruff voice responded.

Dave swung the door open and entered. The smell of flowers filled the air—the ones his captain's wife must have brought, claiming they kept the darkness away from his life. Well, maybe she was onto something, because the captain was generally a fair man who treated his officers right and did his best to make sure they stayed safe. "Good morning, Captain," Dave said.

His boss, who everyone called Captain—sometimes Dave had a hard time remembering his real name—waved him into the visitors' chair facing his desk. "Have a seat."

Captain was a tall man with a boxer's intimidating build and a paunch that showed a love for his wife's cooking, yet his bark was worse than his bite.

A handlebar mustache sat on his face, adding to his charm instead of taking away from it. But his eyes spoke of intelligence that had kept him as the right-hand man of the chief of police for the past three years. It was a mistake to underestimate him.

Dave plopped into the chair and waited for Captain to speak.

"I'm sorry to call you in on your weekend off," Captain began, "but an important case just dropped into our lap, and you might be the best man for it."

Him, Dave, and not a detective under him? He had to hear more. Dave leaned forward as Captain continued speaking. "It's about the Romanov cartel."

An icy chill like from the middle of winter swept over Dave. The Romanov cartel was one of the most violent gangs he'd ever met—they were sadistic just for the fun of it—and the group tied to the only mistake he'd ever made. His boss at the time had confirmed he'd destroyed all of Dave's connections with the cartel. Then how had Captain found out?

"I have my ways," Captain said, as if reading Dave's mind. "I know you don't want to have anything to do with them again, but this may be the big break we've been waiting for to nail those suckers to the wall."

Still… "Can I decline?" If Dave reconnected to

that world, he could lose himself again and, by extension, Zora.

Captain leaned back, his chair creaking, and Dave wondered how long it could hold his large frame before collapsing. "You can, but I hope you won't. We've already lost two fine officers to them."

And I might be the third, Dave mused, *if I go down this road*.

"Their cartel is based in New York, but they've extended their tentacles here, and it's growing worse each day. They've already destroyed many lives," Captain said. "Sure, they've taken a hit, but anything we can do to further bring them down, even in some small way, is worth it." Captain steepled his hands. "Big Mac, the Rooster Head, reached out to say he had some information for us about them. You know him, right?"

Of course, Dave did. But what was Big Mac doing here? He'd been born, bred, and *monstered* in New York. Big Mac was also the one who had helped crack open the wall in the Romanov fortress that enabled Dave to slip in. He'd also saved Dave's life when everything exploded. Dave owed him one. "What does he have to say?" Dave asked.

"He says he'd prefer to meet with our detective on a one-on-one basis," Captain replied.

"Did he request me?"

"No, I doubt he knows you're here now. Just asked for a clean cop he could trust. Since his name came up in your files, I figured you were the best man for it." Captain leaned forward. "We need you to do this, at least for the sake of the officers we've already lost."

Now that he'd put it this way, Dave would seem disloyal if he declined.

"I'm not asking you to go deep undercover," Captain said. "All you need to do is get the information he has and get out. The other detectives will then work on the case. No one else needs to know you were involved, if that's what you'd prefer."

Maybe a quick in and out would work if that was the case. Dave had buried the Romanov cartel in the past, and they needed to stay there. "Okay, I'll do it."

"Great." Captain's face creased into a broad smile. "I'm the only one aware you're on this case, and you'll report to me." He slid a sheet of paper over to Dave. "Here's his contact information. Meet him tonight or tomorrow before he changes his mind and disappears."

"Tomorrow night." Dave needed some time to wrap his mind around what he was about to do.

Captain nodded. "That works for me. I'll tell your

team you're out of town on an urgent assignment." He rose to his feet. Dave did likewise. "Be careful," he said as he extended a hand to Dave.

Dave shook his hand. He had no choice but to be cautious. Otherwise he might bring harm to everyone in his life, including the wonderful Dr. Zora Smyth.

Then he left the office and headed down the hall-way, his hand fiddling with the black key fob recorder he'd been playing with at home before he was called to Captain's office.

10

The smell of roast duck and spice hit Zora's nose as she entered the apartment. It had been a while since she'd been in this place she'd called home and shared with her roommate and best friend Christina for over ten years. Her mom had bought the place in Zora's name when she'd started college, and Zora had never left since then. She'd opted to stay more at her mom's place now that her sister had come back and only returned here on occasional weekends.

She'd repainted the apartment after an intruder had destroyed the place a few months ago, making this its third makeover since Zora had first moved in. Warm pumpkin-colored walls with navy cabinets and stainless steel appliances had now replaced the kitchen's pale mint-green walls with contrasting rich natural wood-grain cabinets and a grey granite countertop. A gold-streaked white granite countertop completed the picture. It was warm and inviting, with a homey vibe, which was what she'd needed after the home invasion.

"Hey, you're back. Just in time." Christina, a beautiful petite redhead, stood in the kitchen stirring a pot of something that smelled heavenly.

Though she might have preferred to spend the day alone, Zora didn't mind having Christina with her. Christina, her soul buddy and ER nurse at Lexinbridge Regional, understood Zora like no one else did. They'd gone through so much together, and yet their friendship had come through unscathed and even much deeper.

"What are you cooking?" Zora said as she approached her. Her stomach growled as the spicy odor hit her nostrils again.

"Hold it right there," Christina said. "I believe you need a shower first? Why don't you take care of that? This spicy ramen noodles with little chunks of roast duck will be hot and ready for you when you come out."

Zora grinned. She'd forgotten she stunk once

she'd inhaled the food aroma. She turned and headed to her bedroom. "I'll be right out."

"You better not stay in there too long if you want a chance at this food. I'm hungry enough for two and can't wait to dig in."

"As if you'd dare," Zora called out as she shut the door of her bedroom behind her. But she hurried out of her clothes and rushed into the bathroom. This was one dare she wasn't willing to bet on.

Seven minutes later, Zora was out of the shower and seated on one of the bar stools at the kitchen countertop, a bowl of piping hot duck ramen noodles in front of her. Just a single bite and she felt like she'd gone to heaven and back, even though her throat and her eyes burned from the spice.

Then Zora remembered the patient who'd died, and her eyes brimmed with the tears she'd tried to hold back all morning. Now they flowed down her cheeks and refused to stop, no matter how much she tried. "Why did you put so much spice into this?" she said between sobs.

"Does it matter at this point?" Christina replied as she sniffled.

Christina must have heard about what had happened, and her best friend, her most wonderful

BFF, had found a way to console her. "Who told you?"

"The hospital grapevine."

Zora shook her head in exasperation. She had to be a celebrity in the grapevine by now, considering how much news they've peddled about her in the last few months. "But how come Brian isn't here? He's just as connected as you are. I'm sure he must have heard about what happened."

"Oh, he wouldn't dare," Christina said in a fierce tone.

Zora gazed at Christina in disbelief. "You guys fought again? Wasn't it like yesterday when you made up?" She'd never seen a couple who broke up and got back together as much as these guys did— they had to hold the Guinness World Record for it— yet she was sure they would walk through fire for each other.

"It's all his fault," Christina said. "There's this new chick that's trying to get her tentacles into him."

"Chick?"

"Well, she's a resident, and her parents and Brian's parents are from the same social circle. Their parents want them to marry each other, but Brian is not interested."

"So, what's the problem?" Zora asked between bites of food.

"Brian hasn't told his parents he isn't interested, though he has told the chick. He says he wants to do it in person. But the chick feels there's some hope since he hasn't informed them. Brian thinks I shouldn't get mad about it, but how can I not? I'm not interested in pretending that I'm okay with the chick and letting her be all over him. If he'd rather go with his parents' wish, then he needs to tell me to my face."

"Christina, you have every right to be mad, but has Brian behaved in any way that shows he's interested in the resident?"

"No, he treats her just like everyone else."

"With what I know about Brian, he might be waiting until he finishes with the board exams, then handling it when that's over. Right now, I don't think he wants to rock the boat with his parents with this most important exam looming in front of him. Why don't you let him know that you'll give him space to handle it until after the exams, and then all bets are off at that point? What do you think?"

"Okay, I hear you. Thanks." Zora made a note to speak to Brian about this situation.

Christina waited for Zora to finish her noodles,

and then they settled on the couch in the living room with a tub of ice cream between them as they watched a cheesy TV show.

"This is the life," Christina said after a while.

Zora raised an eyebrow. "Eating ice cream in the morning?"

"Eating ice cream with my best buddy. It's been a while, with work and everything."

"It's all my fault."

"No, it isn't," Christina said matter-of-factly. "It's just life." She stretched her hands over her head. "I'm just glad you feel better. You do, right?"

"I do."

"Do you want to talk about it?"

"Not right now, but soon. Just don't tell my family about it."

"I won't," Christina promised. "I'm not even sure they'll understand, and it would just stress them out."

"Exactly. Maybe later when I don't feel so emotional about it." Zora yawned.

"Why don't you take a nap, and I'll wake you up later?"

"Thanks. I'll just cuddle up right here on this couch." Zora yawned again, and soon she couldn't keep her eyes open.

A loud cry crashed into Zora's mind, and she opened her eyes. She was in an alley as dark as midnight. The stench of rotten food and urine almost made her gag. Where was she?

A dull light hovered a little distance away, and Zora stumbled toward it.

Then she heard the blood-curdling spine-chilling cry again.

Goosebumps rose on Zora's skin, and cold sweat broke out on her forehead. The cry echoed again and again, and Zora wished she could dash away in the opposite direction as fast as possible.

But she couldn't.

Because the wounded cry sounded somewhat familiar, resonating from deep in her bones.

Soon she reached the light, and Zora could make out a figure huddled on the ground as another figure beat it on its back. Then the figure on the ground turned toward her.

Zora gasped. It was Dave.

A ball of fury grew in her stomach, and Zora rushed forward and pushed away the figure standing over Dave. "Dave, are you alright?" she asked as she wrapped her arms around him. Zora looked up and glared at the figure who'd had the guts to beat Dave.

She felt herself grow cold to the very core of her being as the figure stared back at her.

Her spitting image.

Zora shrieked in horror…

"Zora, wake up!" She could feel a hand rubbing her back. "It's just a nightmare. It's okay."

Zora's eyes flashed opened, and she scrambled away in fright.

"It's just me. Christina. Are you alright?"

The familiar voice brought Zora back to the present, though her heart continued to pound like it could escape her ribcage at any moment. She looked around. She was in her living room and not in some dark alley.

"It's okay. I've got you," Christina said as she approached Zora and then wrapped her arms around her.

Zora soon felt her mind settle and then quiet with Christina's ministrations.

"Do you want to talk about it?" Christina asked.

Zora shook her head. How could she describe what she'd seen?

"That's fine too," Christina said. "How about I make you some of your favorite coffee?" Zora nodded. "Why don't you lie down here? I'll be right back."

Christina stepped away, and soon Zora could hear her puttering about in the kitchen.

Zora tucked a nearby throw pillow under her head. What had that nightmare been all about? She could feel her body shivering just at the thought of it. Did it mean something worse was about to happen, and that Dave would be involved? Was Zora going to harm Dave?

Her phone's ringtone shredded the air.

———

Zora padded back to her bedroom and picked up her phone from the bedside table where she'd left it. She looked at the screen and then swiped the answer button. "Hello, Dave," she said as she perched on the edge of her bed. Was it a coincidence that Dave just called her at this very moment?

"Hey, beautiful. How are you doing?" The sound of his voice warmed her heart and drove away some of the chill from the nightmare.

"Are you drunk?" she said in a teasing tone.

"Only with your love. Just missing you."

Zora laughed. How could he be any more cheesy?

This was what Dave did to her, bringing joy and happiness into her life. There was no way she could hurt him. "Where are you?"

"I'm on a new case."

Something about it chilled her, and her cheerfulness died away. "I thought you were still on the other one," Zora said.

"Yes, I was, but the captain wants me on this instead. He's transferred the other case to another team."

Then Zora remembered the nightmare, and she shivered. "Are you alright?" she asked.

"Yes. Why do you ask?"

"Nothing." How could she tell him she'd dreamed about destroying him? Dave would only worry.

"What about you?" Dave asked. "Are you good?"

"I'm fine."

"Listen, I'm going to be away for a while."

"How long?"

"Just a few days. A week tops."

"Alright. Safe travels."

"I may not leave town. I just…"

"Understood," Zora said. He was going undercover. "But aren't you the lieutenant? Are you expected to be as hands on as before?"

"I'm the only one familiar with this case…"

"Okay. Just be careful." He had to stay safe.

"I will," Dave said. "I'm sorry I can't have dinner with you tomorrow like we'd planned."

"No worries. Just take care of you."

"Will do. I'll call you as soon as I get back. I love you."

"Love you too." Then the line went dead.

Zora dropped the phone beside her. A new assignment. What kind of case was this that needed him to go undercover and on such short notice? She hoped it wouldn't put him in unnecessary danger.

Zora ran her hands through her hair. *Aargh*. The nightmares, the dead patient, Dave's sudden trip undercover—everything was so confusing, and she didn't know what to believe or do. She felt like she'd jumped on a freight train that had picked up speed as it approached a dark tunnel, yet she couldn't stop it. Zora needed help to sort through everything.

So she said a quick prayer and prayed for strength to get through whatever this was. There was no way she could do it on her own, not when she was already sick and tired of every dangerous situation coming to knock at her door.

Soon, a quiet peace and strength filled her heart. Zora remembered how she'd conquered her trials and come out alright. She could get through this, too. Zora wouldn't cower in fear. No matter what had happened or would happen, she was going to face it squarely. She wouldn't hurt or lose Dave like she'd lost Marcus a few months ago, irrespective of what the nightmare showed.

She had no control over what was going on with Dave and his case, but she could start by dealing with the mountain in front of her. First, she would get some much-needed rest, and then she'd begin her preparations for the Morbidity & Mortality conference.

Zora wouldn't let the grief of what had happened crush her.

She'd done the best for her patient, and she was going to prove it.

11

Dave stood close to the mouth of the alley, all dressed in black and hidden in the shadows, and waited. He'd called Big Mac without giving himself away, and they'd agreed to meet here. Even in a neighborhood as run down as this, this alley was avoided because of the horrible, gut-wrenching stench that emanated from it.

The city had replaced and upgraded most of the sewage manholes that spanned the area, but they'd somehow this specific alley, and it still boasted the traditional concrete manhole like some forgotten child, instead of the newer polyethylene kind. The result: the manhole cover had cracked in various spots, releasing odors strong enough to take down a full-grown man on any day. Even washing off the smell didn't help—the scent could linger for days despite many attempts to wash it off. All this meant it was a great meeting spot to avoid eavesdropping ears and eyes.

Dave had arrived a few hours earlier to check out the area and identify potential escape routes if needed. One could never be too careful. Nothing had stuck out, and he was confident he'd get the information he'd come for and be out of the place in only a few minutes. Big Mac didn't like small talk, and neither did he.

He waited and waited and then some more. By this time, the buzzing sound from lingering flies had become too much, even for Dave, but Big Mac never showed up. Only the occasional rat, big enough to take out a toe in one chew, scurried by.

A knot of worry coiled in Dave's stomach. Big Mac had always been a stickler for punctuality. Something or someone must be holding him up if he wasn't here by the agreed time. Dave couldn't go back with no news, so there was only one thing to do.

He had to track Big Mac down.

Dave had triangulated Big Mac's location during their call last night, so he'd spent the rest of the night staking out the nightclub until Big Mac had exited the place. Then he'd followed him until he'd discovered his hideout. Big Mac could have moved places by now, but Dave didn't think he'd do it until after they'd met today. Then he could very well disappear into the wind. Dave's best hope of finding him now was going back to that hideout.

He slunk away from the area, backtracking when needed to avoid being followed. There was something still about the air that made him uneasy, but Dave ignored it, since he had to complete the assignment.

Soon, he arrived at the hole where Big Mac had burrowed. The nondescript house looked like a nineteen-twenties Victorian from an era when folks used to dry their laundry outside, waving and chatting with neighbors as kids ran in the streets and avoided horse-drawn carts. Now, the street was a shadow of itself, with cars that had seen better days parked in front of rundown garages, overgrown lawns filled with junk and other unmentionables, and a quiet atmosphere that seemed primed to explode in violence at a moment's notice.

The house was dark with the curtains drawn, so Dave couldn't tell if anyone was in it. From what he'd remembered, Big Mac liked to operate alone, and that was consistent with what Dave had seen last night. But the house looked a bit more desolate tonight. Something about it triggered Dave's warning bell, but he couldn't go away without some answers. He was sure he'd find something, even if Big Mac wasn't home.

Approaching the front door was out of the question—there was always someone watching in this kind of street. Dave stayed in the shadows as he stepped along the high, overgrown side hedges until he reached the rear of the house. There was a back door, as expected, but it was unlocked and stood ajar.

Strange. The hairs on David's arms stood up straighter, his instincts warning him not to enter. A man like Big Mac would never make this kind of mistake. But if something had gone wrong with him, Dave owed it to him to find out what, so he overrode his reservations and withdrew a pair of black gloves from his jacket pocket and donned them. Then he pulled open the back door as quietly as possible and stepped in.

A strong musty-coated metallic smell hit his nose, and Dave had to force back the cough that threatened to escape his throat. A quick look around the first floor yielded nothing but a neat area. So where was the smell coming from?

Dave treaded up the stairs until he reached the second floor. He checked the two bedrooms on the left; they looked like no one had stepped in them in ages—dust balls and spider webs competed for dominance in each space. Dave was almost certain he'd find nothing of interest in them. That left the room on the right.

As Dave approached it, the smell grew until he recognized it for what it was—the powerful odor of violence, of shed blood that could never return to its origin. He pushed the door open slowly and stepped in with his senses on high alert, only to find a diminutive man spread-eagled on a queen-sized bed with a bullet hole in his forehead. Blood pooled around his head. A black hat with a rooster-head pin lay abandoned on one side of the bed.

It was Big Mac the Rooster Head, deader than dead. Someone had gotten to him before Dave did. Had the Romanov cartel found out he'd been about to snitch and eliminated him? Or had it been another deal gone bad? Those were questions he could explore later; first he had to get out of the house and call his captain.

Dave listened for any other sound as he exited the room, but none reached his ears. He hurried down the stairs, careful not to leave any evidence of his presence behind. As he approached the back door to exit it, bright light flooded the front lawn, its rays piercing through the front windows and in between the curtains into the living room. Men in uniform barged in through the front door with their weapons drawn.

It seemed they hadn't seen him yet. He could still disappear over the fence and exit through a neighbor's lawn.

But the idea died as the back door swung open, and an officer stepped in with his weapon drawn and pointed at Dave's chest.

Dave's eyes widened. "Manny?" Manny had been a friend of the lieutenant whom Dave had replaced. The previous lieutenant had stepped down after they'd exposed his dealings with the mob in Zora's case. Manny wasn't the friendly sort, but he'd always seemed open-minded. "What are you doing here?" Dave asked.

"Let me see your hands, Dave." Manny gestured to another officer, who was now standing behind Dave. "Search him for any weapons."

"Hold on. Manny, what's going on?"

"Search him."

Dave allowed himself to be searched. He hadn't bothered to carry any weapons—he knew martial arts and how to adapt whatever was around him into one. "He's clean," the officer announced.

Dave crossed his arms over his chest. "Manny, what's this?"

Manny pointed down his gun, though he didn't relax his stance. "We got a call that a drug deal and homicide was going down in this house." He turned to the other officers. "Guys, I need you to search the entire house."

A drug deal? Dave was only here to get information, and Big Mac had never been a drug dealer, even in New York. Was this a trap? It was too coincidental they'd come searching the house right after he'd slipped in. His mind found it hard to accept any other option.

"Dave, what are you doing here?" Manny asked, bringing him back to the present.

The captain had stressed the secret nature of his assignment. "What do you mean?"

"You just happen to be in a house where a deal is going down?"

"I don't know about any deal. I need to speak to Captain."

"Captain was the one who sent us."

Dread coiled in Dave's stomach. Captain sent them? Under normal circumstances, Dave wouldn't have worried and might have assumed Captain was the one who'd received the tip. But a superior had burned him, and he no longer believed in coincidences. Yet he hadn't told Captain he'd come here. Unless they'd figured out he would. Had they seen him following Big Mac yesterday? So many questions ran through his mind, but this was not the time to voice them. Dave didn't know what was happening, but he'd hold his reservations about Captain and not expose their operation until he understood what was going on. "I still want to speak to him," he said. "I'd like to make a call."

"Manny, we have a dead body in here," an officer called out from the top of the stairs.

Manny ran a hand through his dirty blond hair. "So the tip was true." He turned to Dave. "Please keep your hands where I can see them."

This was crazy. Was he now a suspect? Most of all, who had killed Big Mac? Did it have anything to do with the captain?

"I found something." Another officer lifted a clear, tightly wrapped package.

"Bring it down here," Manny barked.

The officer, who sported a full head of brown hair, came down the stairs and placed the package on the kitchen counter.

Dave could sense how this would play out, and he didn't like it one bit. It was like they'd choreographed the scene, and he was the puppet set up for the show.

"Open it," Manny ordered.

Dave watched as the officer used a knife and spliced through the packaging. Ten packs of what looked like two pounds each of pure, uncut heroin tumbled out, besides some large prescription drug bottles. The entire package had to be worth five million dollars at a minimum. This was even worse than he'd expected.

"Well, well, well," Manny said. "Who would have thought the great Dave was a dirty cop?"

Dirty cop? Something definitely stunk, and it wasn't him. "This is ridiculous. I know nothing about this."

Manny raised an eyebrow. "Ridiculous? Enough drugs to take down this city is ridiculous? How could you pitch for the bad guys, Dave? I always knew there was something off about you. Dave McKesson, you are under arrest for homicide and drug trafficking and distribution. You have the right to remain silent. Anything you say can and will be used against you in a court of law. You have the right to an attorney. If you cannot afford an attorney, one will be provided for you."

Dave felt hands grab his roughly and pull them behind him. He forced himself not to struggle.

"Sorry, Dave," a voice behind him said as he slapped handcuffs over Dave's wrists. "Just following orders."

This was a mix-up that would be cleared up back at the police station. Hopefully. He had to believe the Captain would resolve this—the alternative was not an option. But for now, he would remain cautious about saying anything that could be used against him.

So Dave stayed quiet, though he remained on high alert as they led him to the squad car.

That was how he noticed the officer who'd found the drugs was no longer on the scene.

The man stood in the shadows, smoking and watching as they led Dave out of the house into the squad car. He'd already changed out of his police uniform and removed his disguise. It'd been too easy blending in and getting the job done.

But this was the best part, watching his victims, like a cat tracked a mouse before pouncing and devouring it.

He'd set the trap.

Now it was time for it to spring.

They took Dave directly to an interview room instead of being fingerprinted, having his picture snapped, and his belongings taken away. Eyes full of disdain and reproach followed him as they led him down the hallway into the room.

The narrow room felt smaller today than all the times Dave had used it to interview suspects, the smell of cigarette smoke and air freshener hanging low in the air. Dave wore a façade that feigned indifference and calm to mask how vulnerable and exposed he felt, knowing the CCTV cameras mounted in the upper corners of the interrogation room captured every twitch and movement of every muscle in his face and body.

Manny sat opposite him but said nothing and refused to look him in the eye. It was as if he was waiting for someone.

The door swung open, and Captain entered. His facial expression was blank, so Dave couldn't tell what he was thinking.

"Manny, step out," Captain ordered.

Manny rose to his feet, threw a disdainful look at Dave, and left the room, shutting the door behind him. Captain settled into the vacated chair.

"How are you doing?" Captain asked.

Dave said nothing. He still wasn't sure if he could trust Captain.

Captain sighed. "You don't have to be careful with me. I have the cameras shut off. Sadie is there to make sure it stays that way." Sadie was the captain's secretary and was formidable enough to stop any officer from butting in. People still speculated, but could never verify, how she'd ended up as his secretary.

But was the recording really off? There was no way to confirm it. He'd had a superior screw him over once before; there was no need to give another boss ammunition to do the same. If he said anything, it had to be something that didn't matter. "What's going on?" he asked.

"I think we have a mole."

Dave's eyes widened. This was the last thing he'd expected to hear. "Why do you think so?"

"Someone must have heard about the assignment and followed you. But why did you go to Big Mac's house? They found enough drugs to give you twenty-five years in the hole, for goodness' sake!"

Easy now. How did Captain know the house belonged to Big Mac? He could very well have been the one tracking Dave. Still, he had to toss Captain a bone that would throw him off the scent of Dave's true feelings about what was going on. Now, how could he do that without incriminating himself? The evade and conquer strategy might work here. "So, what do we plan to do? Am I being charged?"

Captain pinched the top of his nose before letting out a sigh. "I know what you're doing, but I need more information about what you were doing at the house to help you. We're still investigating to find a way out, but things might get worse before they get better."

"What do you mean?"

"You might need to spend some time in lockup. Don't worry, we'll keep you away from the rest of the population. We want whoever is behind all this to think they've got you and show their hand. Then we'll get you out. The situation might not go that far, depending on how everything works out."

This, right here, was a very bad idea. Putting a cop in lockup was like waving meat before a carnivore and telling him not to eat, though Dave didn't plan on being anyone's prey, and if he had his way, he'd climb to the top of the food chain.

He knew better than to rely on the words of his captain. It didn't matter if he was a good guy or a bad guy—there was no way Dave was leaving his future in someone else's hands.

Dave placed his arms on the bolted-down table. "I want a lawyer," he said.

14

Zora spent the rest of the weekend split between prepping for the M & M conference and reviewing some mock exams. It was tiring, but fulfilling. Now all she had to do was deliver her presentation and hope she didn't get any crazy questions. But she was still missing a critical piece of evidence.

Dr. Bennett had informed her yesterday that the preliminary autopsy diagnoses, PAD, was only going to be available early on Monday morning; the full report with detailed microscopic analysis and other studies would be ready in the next two weeks.

As Monday morning dawned bright and clear, Zora paced in front of the pathologist's office as she waited for him to arrive. She needed this report like a dog needed a bone. If her presentation covered the hypotheticals about what had happened with the case, the report contained the evidence that revealed its truth.

She looked at her watch; it was almost time for the conference. If the pathologist didn't appear soon, what was she going to do? Zora said a quick prayer and wrung her hands together as she waited.

A young man in his thirties approached the office next door with a sheet of paper in his right hand and a briefcase in his left. Fortunately, Zora had looked up the pathologist's profile in the hospital directory—Dr. Bennett had given her the name—before coming here. "Good morning, Dr. Collins," Zora said.

The man turned to her, pale blue eyes scrutinizing her face. "Do I know you?" he asked.

"Dr. Bennett sent me to pick up the preliminary autopsy report for Oliver Young."

"Ah, you're Dr. Smyth. Dr. Bennett said you would be by."

Zora wished she could make small talk, but this was not the time for it—she had to be at the confer-ence in the next ten minutes. "I hope you don't mind—"

"Of course, you must be in a hurry," he said, a tinge of disappointment in his voice.

Pathologists loved to discuss their work and how they'd arrived at their conclusion, and Zora wasn't letting him have his fun. She wanted to reassure him she would be back, but she couldn't afford to make any promises, not with how busy her schedule was. But she could try to come back when the full report came out.

"Thanks for understanding," Zora said instead.

Dr. Collins looked at her and then chuckled. "You're certainly different," he said. He thrust the sheet of paper he'd been holding into her hand. "Here you go. Cause of death was cardiac arrest secondary to peripheral vasodilation and myocardial ischemia from anaphylaxis. Causative agent is still under investigation. Tell Dr. Collins he'll get the electronic version later this morning."

Zora's eyes widened. "Are you saying an NMBA did not cause the anaphylaxis?"

Dr. Collins' eyes twinkled. "We still need to run some more tests to provide a conclusive report. But," he pointed his finger upward as if he was in a class teaching his student, "he definitely died from complications of anaphylaxis."

"Alright. Thank you, Dr. Collins."

"You're welcome. Now, off you go."

Zora didn't hesitate and hurried toward the hospital's main building. She glanced at her watch. She had five minutes to make it there on time.

Otherwise, everything she'd worked so hard for might go up in smoke.

Zora stepped out of the conference room with Brian by her side. The Morbidity & Mortality conference had gone much better than she'd expected. Her peers and senior colleagues in the surgery department had agreed her treatment protocol was in line with the expected standard of care. They'd rendered a judgement that the case was non-preventable, with a recommendation to the hospital leadership that no further action was necessary in the case.

Herbert's case had been deemed preventable, so the department had recommended physician education, monitoring of his subsequent patient care, and mandatory additional training for him, though Zora doubted if anything would come of it. Brian didn't think so either—he'd heard that Herbert had deep connections with someone in the hospital leadership, even if he didn't know who.

"Great work, Zora," Brian said. "It validates what

I already knew: that you'd done your best for the patient."

"I'm relieved they agreed with me. But a man died. I have to learn a lot more to prevent this from ever happening again."

"And you will, in time."

Just then, someone brushed roughly past Zora, hitting her shoulder and knocking her off center.

Zora felt a sharp ache in her shoulder, and she whirled to see who the culprit was. Of course, who else could be so rude but Herbert the hulk? "Hey!"

Brian's hand on her arm held her back. "Let him go. It's not worth it."

"I wasn't planning to," Zora said. "But it would have been nice to get an apology."

Brian watched Herbert go. "His ego must be so bruised right now after getting all that criticism and feedback from his peers and colleagues."

"If only it would be enough to get him to wake up and change his ways. You know, it would have been different if he made an effort to learn and improve."

"I know. Anyway, where are you off to now?" Brian asked.

"A mini-round to see my patients."

"Just make sure you don't forget our meeting this evening. I got us a room."

"A room? Brian, what are you thinking?"

Brian's eyes widened. "Oh please, get your mind out of the gutter. Have you forgotten that we agreed to review practice questions for the boards today?"

"Oh, right."

Brian chuckled. "Dr. Gaines has given us permission to use his office. That way, I can remain close to the ER in case I'm paged." Dr. Gaines was Brian's attending and mentor.

Zora remembered when she'd once had someone like him, but Dr. Edwards had betrayed and kidnapped her instead, and then been murdered. She shook her head mentally. There was no need dwelling on such morbid thoughts. "Okay, I'll be there. It's seven p.m., right?"

"Yes. I've also arranged some takeout from your favorite Italian restaurant."

The thought of food from Giovinni made her stomach growl—she'd only had coffee so far today. "Oooh, nice. I'll have to leave by ten p.m., though. Tomorrow is a long day with clinic and everything, and I need to get some quality sleep tonight."

"Zora, you're the only one I know who speaks of quality sleep this close to the boards. Everyone else is running around like chickens with their heads cut off. I guess it's because you've always scored in the ninetieth percentile on the ABSITEs." The ABSITEs were the annual in-training examinations from the American Board of Surgery that general surgery residents had to take each year of their residency program.

"But you're just as good," Zora countered.

Brian shook his head. "I have to crack my head open and dump the information into it, whereas you seem to just coast through. Please teach me your ways, oh wise one."

Zora chuckled. "Oh, please." She checked her time. "I'll see you later. And make sure you call Christina and make up with her. I'm tired of being your go-between."

"But there's no need for a go-between, darling. That relationship is on a hiatus until the boards are over."

"Then tell her, for goodness' sake. Oh wait! So you admit you're both in a relationship," Zora teased. "I never know what you guys are."

"Zora, isn't that your patient's mother behind you?"

"Who?" She looked behind her to see who Brian was talking about, but there was no one there. Zora turned back, but Brian was already making a speedy exit toward the ER.

She laughed and shook her head. Those two. When would they grow up? She continued smiling as she turned to head toward the surgical unit.

Then her smile froze and disappeared.

Standing far off and staring at Zora with hate-filled eyes was Oliver Young's mother.

Zora's heart skipped a beat. What was she going to do? She must have seen Zora laughing and assumed she'd forgotten about her dead son already, which was far from the truth. How could she handle this without it blowing up in her face? Zora could pretend she didn't see the woman, or she could go right up to her.

She chose the latter—she had nothing to hide. But then the woman was no longer standing there.

Zora hurried to where she'd stood and searched for her, but she'd disappeared into thin air. It was as if Oliver's mother had never been there.

Realizing it was futile to keep searching for her, Zora made for the cafeteria to grab a bite before heading back to her original destination.

But something told her, from the look in Oliver's mother's eyes, that it wasn't over.

Zora stood in front of the elevators on the ground floor and waited for one to arrive. The entire area buzzed with activity as patients, their caregivers, and hospital staff rushed past her in various directions, intent on their destinations. The heady smell of flowers from the surrounding gardens wafted in through the central revolving door, blending with the strong antiseptic smell so pervasive in all hospitals.

She'd spent more time than she'd planned on grabbing something to eat, and now Zora was running behind if she wanted to clear the to-dos on her plate before her meeting with Brian tonight.

The elevator pinged, and the doors slid open. She

stepped in and scanned the messages on her phone while she waited for it to close.

"Zora! Wait up!"

Zora looked up. *That sounded like Christina's voice.* She stretched out her hand between the elevator doors to stop it from closing, and they pulled back. "Sorry," she said to the other occupants of the elevator as she stepped out.

"I've been looking for you," Christina said, drawing to a halt. Her chest heaved as she tried to gulp in more air. "It's Dave."

Zora's heart raced. "What about him?"

"They've arrested him!"

Zora's heart nosedived, and she reached out for the closest wall to steady herself. *No, no, no! How?* The memory of his cry from the nightmare flashed before her. It couldn't be. It had to be a mistake. He was a cop, for goodness' sake, and he'd been on a case. How had he gone from that to an arrest? "How?"

"It's all over the news." Zora's knees weakened, and she stumbled. "Zora!"

No, this was all a lie. He was supposed to be undercover for a case, and Dave had never lied to her before. How could they have arrested him? The whole thing smelled fishy.

She took a deep breath and forced herself to straighten. *Pull yourself together, Zora.* She had to stay strong, calm, and alert to help him.

Something was very wrong here, and Zora was going to do whatever it took to get to the truth. "Let's go," she said.

Captain paced back and forth across his office. His mind whirled as he tried to figure out a plan, but none was forthcoming. How had it deteriorated to this? This wasn't supposed to happen!

It was supposed to be a straightforward case: he'd get the evidence against the Romanov cartel, wrap it up in a bow, and present it to the chief like an offering for sacrifice. The chief would ride off to his retirement in glory, and Captain would take his place, fulfilling his long-awaited dream of becoming the chief of police for Lexinbridge PD, with more than enough money to support his wife's burgeoning shoe and flower addictions. Now everything seemed to have backfired, with the additional headache of dealing with the public's outcry against a dirty cop, which wouldn't have happened in the first place without this case.

He pinched the bridge of his nose. Had someone used him to get to Dave? The thought didn't sit well with him. He should have listened to his gut when he'd received the information about Dave's history with the Romanov cartel—his instincts had warned him it had been too easy.

Captain had also thought the anonymous tip about the drug deal would help catch one of the Romanov boys in the act. He hadn't known Dave would be there. What had he been doing there, anyway? Now, he wasn't even sure if he should believe Dave had cut ties with the Romanovs, or if he just gave the illusion that he'd done so. Was he the one who'd killed Big Mac, or had a puppet master behind the scenes arranged it?

Then, to make matters worse, Manny had gone off the script. He was only supposed to arrest the bad guys. Why had he then arrested Dave when he hadn't even caught him in the act? Was this revenge against Dave for the former lieutenant's dismissal from the force? This would have never made the news if Manny had only brought Dave in for a chat with Captain. Captain wasn't sure who was telling the truth or who was lying, but he had to clean up this mess before it deteriorated any further.

There was a knock on his door.

Captain halted. "Come in," he responded.

Manny entered his office, his eyes looking everywhere but at Captain. "Captain, I don't—"

"What the hell happened?" Captain barked.

Manny tucked his hands behind his back. "No idea, Captain. I don't know how the media found out about it."

Really, Manny? That's your excuse? "If you hadn't arrested Dave in the first place, then the media wouldn't have mattered!" Manny shrunk back at Captain's outburst.

Captain ran a hand through his short bushy hair and then pointed a finger at Manny. "I don't care how you're going to do it, but you are going to fix this! The chief is all over my head about it, and you know how he gets when he's mad. You have twenty-four hours to make it happen. And find that snitch!"

Manny nodded vigorously. "Yes, sir!"

"Now get out of my office."

Manny turned and hurried out as if his pants were on fire.

Captain rubbed his forehead. Now he had a full-blown headache to deal with.

His eyes spotted the flowers his wife had brought in this morning, and he frowned. Captain grabbed them and dumped them in the trash can.

He had to contain this problem, and he had to do it fast.

Otherwise, he'd have no choice but to watch the ship of his promotion sail away.

17

"**B**oss, you need to see this." One of Lucas' boys who shared his cell rushed over to where Lucas sat on the lower bunk bed, holding the newspaper a CO had delivered this morning.

"What is it?" Lucas asked.

"Here, boss." His boy pointed to an article.

Lucas scanned the newspaper for a moment.

Then he burst out laughing, almost doubling over. The great and mighty Dave, all knocked down! Who would have thought it'd be this easy? The years he'd waited and the money he'd paid the guy had been worth it. *Aaah!* Revenge was so sweet. The only thing he regretted was he wasn't there to see the bastard's face as he squirmed.

Lucas' hand squeezed the paper until it was almost crushed. He would not rest until he had Dave's life squeezed out of him. His sister should have been alive now, if not for Dave, buying up everything in the stores like she'd loved to do. Instead, Lilianna was buried six feet under, her bright innocent face gone from him forever. She'd taken the bullet for that bastard who'd betrayed the family, because of that useless thing called love.

The muscles of his jaw twitched as he crushed his teeth together. What Dave had experienced so far wasn't yet enough. He had to feel the ache of what it meant to lose a loved one like Lucas had.

Lucas tossed the paper to his minion. "Burn it."

The man caught the paper and hurried to the attached stainless steel toilet, blocking the view while he set the paper on fire with a match, the shadows of the flame flickering against the dull cream-colored walls of the cell. Lucas watched until it burned to ashes and was then flushed away.

He stretched and laid back on his bed.

That was how he planned to deal with Dave.

Lucas was going to destroy him until there was nothing left of him.

18

Zora pulled out her phone and made a call as she hurried with Christina out of the hospital. "Hey, Brian," she said.

"Missing me already?" Zora heard from the other end of the line.

Zora chuckled. "You're crazy." Then her tone turned serious. "Listen, I need your help."

"What is it?"

"Dave is in trouble, and I need to be there for him. Could you help me check in with my patients to make sure they're alright and watch over them for the next few hours?"

"I hope Dave is alright. Take all the time you need. I'll even hand them over to the night team on your behalf once it's time. I'm on call in the hospital anyway, so they can reach me anytime."

"Thank you. I'll send their names to you and let my resident know he can reach out to you if he needs anything. Sorry about missing tonight's meeting."

"No problem. We can do the mock exam some other day. Just send me a text update about Dave, okay?"

"I will. Thanks." Zora ended the call.

She headed to the valet station and handed over some cash and the valet card. Then she dialed another number while she waited. "Hello, Silas." Silas was her mom's fellow partner at the law firm and also her boyfriend. He was a well-known criminal lawyer in the city as well.

"Zora! How are you doing?"

"Good. Where are you?"

"At your mom's place. She's working from home today."

"Could you meet me at the police station?"

"Why?" His voice turned serious. "Are you in trouble?"

"No, it's Dave. I think he needs our help."

"I'll be there in about ten minutes."

"Thanks, Silas." The call ended.

"Doc, your car is here," the guy at the valet

station said as he handed back one-half of the valet card and a receipt to her.

"Thank you." Zora and Christina walked over to where another valet waited with her car.

"What did Silas say?" Christina asked.

"He'll meet us at the station." At the look on Christina's face: "You don't have to go. I could drop you off at the apartment if you'd like."

"Could you? I still get the shivers when I go to the police station."

Zora understood. Christina had spent some unpleasant hours at the police station a few months ago, and going there would remind her of what had happened. Zora had been the same way too, after all she'd been through.

But this was Dave, and she would do anything to help him.

"Alright. Let's get going," she said.

"Thanks for coming, Silas," Zora said. They were standing next to where Silas had parked outside the police station. Silas was immaculately dressed, as usual.

The warm sun shone down, yet it wasn't enough

to fend off the chill she always got from being this close to this squat brick building. The air was crisp, yet to Zora, it felt polluted and poisonous, prompting a desire in her to flee as far away from this place as possible.

She squelched the impulse. Dave needed her.

"Always happy to help," Silas said. "I heard about the case on the radio on my way here. It doesn't look good, since it seems they arrested him at the house where everything had happened. That's enough to connect him to the crime."

Zora's heart sank. "Is there anything you can do?"

Silas patted her shoulder. "Don't worry. I'll do the best I can to get him out."

"Thank you."

"Why don't you wait in your car? I'll come and meet you once I'm done."

"Okay."

Zora moved to her car and watched as Silas entered the station. She slipped into the car, sent up a quick prayer, and then waited.

Dave was innocent no matter what anyone said, and she would not stand by and let him end up rotting in jail.

Not on her watch.

"Oh, my goodness. Thank you, God," Zora said as she rushed forward and hugged Dave. He looked disheveled after spending the night at the station, but she didn't care. She was just glad they'd released him. "Thank you, Silas."

"My pleasure."

"How did you get him out?"

"Let's just say I had some straight talk backed by some pertinent information with his captain after speaking with Dave. But the case is still open." Silas looked around. "I think it might be best to move this reunion to your mom's home. We don't want any reporters taking pictures."

"You're right. I'll take Dave in my car and we'll meet you there."

"Sounds good. See you soon." Silas headed to his car, while Zora led Dave to where she'd parked. Soon they were on their way.

The ride home was quiet. Dave's eyes were closed as he leaned back in his seat. But it didn't bother Zora—she was comfortable giving him whatever he needed in the moment.

Finally, Dave broke the silence. "Thanks for coming to get me out."

Zora gave him a warm smile. "My pleasure. Are you okay?"

Dave nodded. He was quiet for another moment. "I didn't do it," he said.

"Sure. I believe you."

He turned his head to catch her eyes. "You do?"

"Why wouldn't I? I know you, Dave. You wouldn't kill someone in cold blood, not without a legitimate reason, and you don't do drugs."

"Thanks for the vote of confidence," he said quietly. "But I haven't always done everything on the up and up."

Zora had guessed at some underlying PTSD from his undercover days after hearing him muttering in his sleep. He'd had a nightmare during one of his naps at her place. She hadn't brought it up, figuring he'd talk to her whenever he was ready. Maybe things had gone wrong during that time, and he'd made mistakes, but that didn't make him a killer.

"Maybe you haven't, but isn't that expected when you're undercover?" Zora said. "Oh, don't look at me like that. I'm not an idiot. If you ever made a mistake, it would have been while you were under-cover. But you're a good man, Dave. I'm not one to be attracted to bad boys." She winked at him. Dave laughed. "Nice to hear that wonderful laughter again," she said.

"You're a hoot, you know that?" Dave said.

Zora flashed him a smile. "Absolutely. And you're welcome." Then she turned serious. "But why do I feel you're being set up this time around? Something struck me wrong about it when you first mentioned you had a new case."

Dave gave her a sharp look. "You think so too?"

"Sure. You're a cop. They should have given you the benefit of a doubt when they found you at the guy's house. Instead, they arrested you, and before it's even daybreak, it's already on the news. If that doesn't stink, then I don't know what does."

Dave let out a sigh. "I don't know who's behind it, but I'm going to find out."

"You mean *we*'re going to find out. I'm not letting you do this alone. We, all of us, my family and I, are going to help you figure this one out."

"No, Zora. I can't put your family at risk."

"Let us do this for you, Dave. You've always been there for me, and I want to do the same for you."

"But it's dangerous, and you have your boards coming up soon. That's all you need to focus on right now. It has been a big dream of yours to become a board-certified surgeon, and I won't forgive myself if we mess that up too."

"If anyone is going to mess it up, it won't be you. Oh, don't give me that look. Nothing is going to happen. I'll study and do everything I need to do to be ready for the exams, and I won't do anything dangerous."

"Promise?"

"On Scout's honor," Zora said.

"Since when?"

"Since when what?"

"Were you a Scout?"

"That's not the point. But accept my family's help at least. They're lawyers and are used to your world."

Dave laughed and shook his head. "Okay, I'm going to close my eyes and take a nap."

"What? You can't leave me hanging!"

He gave her a lazy smile. "I love you, Zora."

Zora's heart melted at his words. No matter what he said, she would never let him do this alone. "We're here." She parked in front of the house.

Zora laughed as Dave groaned.

Dave shut the door behind them as they entered the foyer of Zora's mom's home, also known as the family house. It had surprised Zora to see a security team already in place around the house. Her mom must have called them in after Zora had reached out to Silas for help.

Zora led Dave through the foyer lined with her late father's watercolor paintings. This home was where Zora had been born and raised, but she'd limited her stay after she'd moved out for college, to avoid the pain of facing life here without her sister and dealing with a withdrawn mother.

Thankfully, her relationship with her mom had improved so much that their issues before seemed only like a bad dream. Her sister coming back had been the icing on the cake. Their home was now bubbling with love and laughter again.

"Oh my goodness, Dave!" Her mom, Adrianna Smyth, hurried over with Silas at her heels. "How are you doing?" She grabbed his arm and led him through the foyer and into the living room.

"I'm fine, ma'am," he responded.

"I'm glad you're okay." Her mom settled Dave on the large brown leather sofa in the living room, while Zora sat on his other side.

"I need to take a few calls," Silas said. "I'll be in

the home office. We can talk about our next steps later."

"Sounds good," Dave said. "Thanks again."

"My pleasure," Silas said. He gave her mom a peck and then headed toward the double French doors that led to the other section of the house.

Her mom patted Dave's hand. "Alisa, get Dave something to drink."

Alisa was curled up on one of the smaller couches with a magazine in her hands, looking as gorgeous as any model with those beautiful cheekbones and delicate features. She got up and went into the kitchen without saying a word to anyone and returned a minute later with a glass of water. She handed it to Zora.

"Here you go," Zora said as she passed the glass to Dave.

"Thank you."

Zora turned to her sister, who'd returned to her couch. "Aren't you supposed to be at work?"

"I'm at work. I'm working today with mummy dearest."

Zora's eyes swung back to her mom. "What's going on with her?" Zora whispered.

Her mom shrugged. "I don't know. She was fine a minute ago. I pulled her in today to work on a case with me." She took the now empty glass from Dave and dropped it on the coffee table. "So how can we help you get through this?" she asked Dave.

Zora fought back a smile. Trust her mom to hit the nail on the head. *Babe, let's see how you'll dodge this*, she thought.

"I'll take care of it, ma'am," Dave said.

"It's not up for discussion," her mom replied. "This is what family does. We help each other. You're family." Alisa snorted. "Young lady, what was that?"

"He can clearly take care of it," Alisa said. "Why do we have to help?"

"Alisa!" Zora snapped, rising to her feet. "What's wrong with you?"

Alisa uncurled from where she lay. "Me? You should ask him that. Who are you really, Mr. Dave?"

"What do you mean?" Zora said in a frozen tone.

"He knows what I'm referring to. Don't you, Detective McKesson?"

Dave pulled Zora's arm to get her to sit down. "It's okay, Zora. Let it go."

"No, it's not okay. I'm sick and tired of how she's been treating you. Alisa, I want you to apologize."

Alisa jumped to her feet, her face grim. "I'll do no such thing. If you help him, it's going to come back and bite you in the butt, mark my words." With that, she strode away and headed up the stairs.

Zora watched her sister in disbelief. Why was she being so dramatic when she knew very well that Zora needed her support? She sat back on the couch. "I'm sorry, Dave," she said.

"It's not a big deal. Even though I don't understand why she doesn't like me, you should go up and make up with her once I'm gone. She's your sister and loves you very much."

"Gone?" Zora's mom said. "You're going nowhere, young man. You'll spend the next few days here until we have this issue sorted."

"Thanks for the offer, but there's no need," Dave said.

"I insist."

Zora nudged Dave and nodded her head. There was no arguing with her mom once she'd made up her mind. It was best Dave saved his energy.

"Thank you, ma'am," he said quietly.

"You're welcome."

Zora leaned back. "Mom, I see you've already engaged the security team." Zora had met them on their way in.

"Absolutely. We can't take any chances, and I'll sleep better knowing they are here to keep intruders out." Dave fought a yawn. "Why don't you go use the guest room upstairs, the one you've stayed in before, to freshen up?" her mom said to him. "You can grab a nap if you like."

"Thanks, ma'am. I'll take you up on that offer." He turned to Zora and kissed her forehead. "I'll talk to you later."

Zora nodded and gave him a warm smile. Then she watched as he made his way upstairs and disappeared into the room.

The doorbell rang at that moment.

"Now who could that be?" Her mom rose and padded to the door. Zora heard it being opened and then shut. "Oh my goodness."

Zora got to her feet. "What is it, Mom?" She hurried to where her mom stood with an envelope in her hands.

Her mom lifted her eyes to Zora, her face pale. "You're about to be sued."

19

Alisa smashed her face into the pillow as she lay on her princess-style ornate bed with its pink-tufted headboard, which meshed well with the seafoam green walls boasting watercolor paintings by her late father.

Aargh. What was she thinking? She'd practically announced to Dave that she was onto him. Now he would cover his tracks. *Alisa, how could you be so stupid?* she thought.

She hadn't planned to blow up and throw a tantrum like a teenager. But the combination of Dave pretending to be innocent, Zora fawning over him, and her mom treating him like a son-in-law had prompted her outburst. The hypocrisy of it all had disgusted Alisa.

Yet she felt bad. It wasn't Zora's fault, and she'd taken out her anger on her. Maybe she'd apologize to her later.

She lifted her head and rolled onto her back. Charles had told her the report would be ready in a week, but Alisa wished she'd get it sooner. She needed to expose Dave for the fraud he was before he wrapped his tentacles more tightly around Zora and dragged her family through the mud.

She reached into her nightstand's drawer and pulled out the burner phone. Maybe she should call Charles now.

No. There were only a few days left till Charles would have the report ready. Showing her impatience would only reveal how desperate she was. It was better to wait until then.

If she was truthful to herself, a part of her wished for Zora's sake that the man she'd seen that fateful day was all a mirage and not the Dave sitting downstairs in their living room.

Because Alisa would tear him apart bit by bit if he were one and the same.

Only four more days, and then the wait would be over and the truth revealed.

20

"How the hell did this happen?" Lucas shouted from the other end of the line. "They've released McKesson, and the news about him has all but disappeared!"

The man's jaw twitched. This reaction was just what he'd anticipated from the pompous bastard. "It was unexpected," the man responded in a languid tone.

"Well, fix it." The line clicked dead.

The man grunted. It was idiots like this Lucas that sometimes made his work tedious. How could he doubt the man who'd helped topple regimes as far away as in Africa? Taking care of Detective McKesson was nothing compared to that. Patience was the name of the game. What a fool this Lucas was. It'd been a mistake to take the job.

He'd only done it because he'd been bored and needed a change of pace. The man didn't need the money; he had more than enough in banks around the world to last him seven lifetimes.

Nevertheless, he'd keep his own end of the bargain like he always did. He even had some wonderful surprises all set up for Detective McKesson.

The man picked up his joint from the ashtray on his desk, placed it in his mouth, leaned back, and blew out a ring of smoke into the air.

Let the games continue.

21

"**W**hat?" Zora snatched the envelope from her mom's hands.

Her mom recovered quickly. "It's a notification from the estate of a Mr. Oliver Young of the intent to sue you for the wrongful death of Oliver Young. Zora, what's this about?" As Zora stared at the open flap, her mom said, "Sorry, I opened it without your permission."

Zora shook her head. "No worries. You're my lawyer, after all." She pulled the letter from the envelope and scanned it. *Not this.*

"Zora, what's going on?" her mom asked.

"Oliver Young was a patient of mine who passed away on the operating table this last weekend, despite everything we did to save his life. My department even had a mortality conference today on his case, just like we do for all deaths regarding patients under our care, and all the surgeons agreed that my treatment protocol was more than adequate for the patient. So this," she shook the letter in her hand, "is just ridiculous."

"Silas!" her mom called out in a loud voice. "I need you here!" She turned to Zora, "Come on. Let's sit down and talk about it."

Zora followed her mom back to the couch. It was just the absolute worst timing for this. She now had this ridiculous lawsuit looming over her, just when Dave needed her help, and not counting her board exams that were around the corner.

Silas appeared a moment later, his button-down shirt sleeves all rolled up. "What's going on?" he asked.

"Take a seat," her mom said. "We have business to discuss. Zora is about to be sued."

Silas looked from her mom to Zora. "What?"

"Here." Zora handed him the letter.

Silas read the letter and then looked up. "I need to call in an expert. Hold on one second." He pulled his phone from his pant pocket and dialed a number. Then he placed it on speakerphone. "Richard! How are you? I have you on speaker. Adrianna Smyth is here as well as her daughter, Dr. Zora Smyth."

"Hello, Adrianna," a deep voice said. "It has been a while."

"Good to speak to you again, Richard. How's Miranda?"

"On my case, as usual." He bellowed out a laugh. "You know how she's always 'encouraging' me to lose weight."

"I'm on her side on this one," her mom said. "You need to be around to see your grandkids."

"Well, that would only happen if I could get the boy to marry. He's too picky, that one. Anyway, to what do I owe the honor of this call?"

"Dr. Smyth here is about to be sued in a wrongful death suit," Silas answered. "I need your help here as the expert."

"They're going after the young ones now? You know what? Why don't I send my son over? He's now more an expert in this than I am."

"Oh please, who could ever beat you?" her mom said. "You're a titan in this area."

Richard chuckled. "My heart thanks you for the nice boost, Adrianna." Then his voice turned serious. "I can send AJ over now."

"That would be great," Silas said. "I'll text you the address."

"Good luck. Especially you, Dr. Smyth."

"Thank you, sir," Zora chimed in.

"I have to go. Miranda is calling my name. I imagine she's brought some chicken to entice me to get on the treadmill."

"Bye, Richard," Silas said. The line went dead. Silas picked up the phone and shot off a text message before slipping it back into his pocket. "So, while we wait for AJ, why don't we grab a bite in the kitchen? I bought some salads from your mom's favorite Thai restaurant on my way here. I have a feeling this is going to be a long meeting."

"Hello, I'm Andrew Beckett, also known as AJ," the stylish young lawyer said as he extended his hand to Zora. "Nice to meet you."

Zora shook his hand. "Nice to meet you, too. I'm Dr. Zora Smyth." His hand warmed her skin, just like the smile on his face. "Please sit." She gestured at an available seat by her side at the dining table. They'd moved there for more privacy. Silas sat next to her mom, while Zora sat opposite her.

"Thanks for coming at such short notice, AJ," Silas said.

"It's my pleasure, sir."

"Would you like anything?" her mom asked.

"Maybe a glass of water."

Zora pushed back her seat and stood to her feet. "Coming right up." She could feel AJ's eyes on her as she made her way to the kitchen. She'd seen the spark of interest in his eyes, but he was professional enough not to make it obvious. Thank goodness for that, since she only had eyes for Dave.

She pulled a bottle of spring water from the refrigerator and placed it on a tray with a glass. Then she carried the items into the dining area. "Here you go," she said as she placed the tray in front of him. "Would you like me to open it for you?"

"No, thank you," he reassured her. "I'll do it myself." He poured some water into the glass and drank half of it before placing the glass back on the tray. Then he looked around the table. "Can we get started?" He turned to Zora. "Why don't you tell us what happened? Please tell us everything, even those you think might be inconsequential."

"Okay."

Zora told them what happened on Saturday morning, both in the ER and the OR. "The preliminary autopsy results show death from cardiac arrest triggered by anaphylaxis, though the causative agent is currently unknown. They plan to have the final report available within two weeks."

"Hold on. You mean the patient just died this weekend, and they already intend to sue you?" AJ asked in a disbelieving tone.

"Yes. Why?"

AJ folded his arms across his chest. "There's a significant amount of work involved behind the scenes before a plaintiff sues. The plaintiff's lawyer needs to speak with the plaintiff and any related parties about the details of the case, investigate its facts, and seek expert opinion about the potential viability of the claim. Then they need to set up an estate at the court where the deceased lived. The attorney may also try to reach out to your malpractice insurance company to see if the potential claim is subject to any coverage."

"The state does not require residents to carry malpractice insurance," Zora said.

"Good to know. Yet all that is a lot of work to accomplish in two days, which also happens to fall over the weekend when the courts are closed. This process sometimes takes weeks or months, so you can imagine how this is unusual."

It was. "Do you mean they might have planned this ahead of time?" Zora asked.

"That's a strong possibility. We'll keep our minds open at this point."

If it was pre-planned, did it mean they'd set her up? Who could be behind it if that was the case? Of course, Zora had enemies, but not any that would be desperate to take her down.

"But they need to prove you breached the standard of care either through something you've done wrong or something you omitted to do that any reasonable surgeon would do, by engaging expert witnesses who would speak to that," AJ continued. "They also need to prove that the breach resulted in an injury to the deceased. Finally, they need to convince a jury that the injury resulted in damage to the plaintiff, quantifying what the dollar amount would be. But from what you've just told me, this should be a tough case for them to find issues with, since it would be hard to prove you breached any standard of care."

"Correct. What's bugging me most is that I don't think they have any concrete evidence to support their claim."

"Unless they're manufacturing one. Which begs

the question: on what basis are they pursuing this claim?"

"That's what I'd like to know," Zora stated.

"One question though: was the attending in the OR from the beginning to the end?"

Zora shook her head. "No, he wasn't, though I spoke to him about the case before the surgery, and I called him in as soon as I realized we had an issue on our hands. Would that be a problem?"

"That can be an angle they might use," AJ said.

"But fifth-year surgical residents are in charge of their patients and have final responsibility for their care."

"But not legally," AJ said. "The law only recognizes the attending as having the final say. But that doesn't mean we can't use that as an argument to rebut that position. Do you have bylaws about this?"

"We have a residents' manual put together by the hospital that outlines the responsibilities of residents by year."

"That would work too."

"Okay."

"I'm also concerned that they've hired Schyzman and Schyzman. That's a very expensive law firm to employ. How is the plaintiff able to afford them? It's not like they're the kind to do pro bono work."

"I agree," her mom said. "And they love to bill. Don't give me that look, Zora. All lawyers love to bill, but Schyzman and Schyzman are in a class of their own for that, so their fees end up typically astronomical. Now, they could decide they want to get paid after they win the lawsuit, but they would do that only if the probability of winning the case is high, which I'm assuming won't be in this scenario. So why would Schzman take this case? Something is not adding up."

Zora rubbed her forehead. Just thinking about this case was already giving her a headache. "So what now?"

"If you choose to hire us, we'll start pulling together all the documents and evidence we need for the case. Any information you can provide without breaking HIPPA laws would be helpful. We'll also begin investigations into the background of the plaintiff to understand who we're dealing with and what's going on here. Also, the notice you received today should trigger pre-suit settlement negotiations between both parties."

"I have no plans to settle," Zora said. "I did nothing wrong."

"Remember that a settlement is not an admission of negligence, but an attempt to cut losses," AJ said.

"Yet it would go on my record and has to be reported to the state medical board, and I don't want that, when it's obvious I've done nothing wrong. I won't settle."

"Okay. However, keep in mind that negotiations are also a way to find out what the plaintiff's attorneys have up their sleeves, so it can be very helpful," AJ stated.

"What's the average settlement for this type of case these days?" her mom asked.

"It's a wide range. Anywhere from several hundred thousand dollars to tens of millions of dollars, but these types of cases are usually tough for plaintiffs to win and can take anywhere from two to five years to resolve. That's why we like to go in strong in the beginning and nip it in the bud.

"Now, Dr. Smyth, there are a couple more things you should be mindful of: you should not speak to anyone about this case. This includes friends, co-workers, your attending, and the plaintiff's family or related parties. Even the hospital. You should have a lawyer with you for any discussion with the hospital. We don't need a 'he said, she said' situation."

"Got it," Zora said.

"Also, residents don't get immunity in this state and are thus subject to liability for their negligence or omission, which means the plaintiff can sue you. Even though we expect the attending to be named in the lawsuit as well, the hospital and their insurance company will not allow the attending to admit responsibility for you until after the statute of limitations for this case has expired, which is two years from the date the deceased passed away. So basically, you're on your own."

Yikes. That sounded awful.

"I'll cover the costs for everything," her mom said.

"You don't need to do that, Mom. I still have my inheritance." Her dad had left her a generous legacy that had only grown over the years, which was a relief because there was no way Zora could afford a lawsuit on her meagre salary alone. Only attendings and above earned the big bucks.

"That money is for your future, like opening your own practice or buying an island."

"An island? Mom, this isn't the time for a joke."

"Of course, you can buy an island." Her mom grinned. "Just pulling your legs, honey. But seriously, I'll handle the fees. Let me do that for you."

"Alright. Thanks."

"You're welcome."

"So, Dr. Smyth, how are you feeling about everything?" AJ asked.

Zora leaned back. "Ambushed."

"I know this might be a big blow to your confidence, but it's important to remember that this could have happened no matter how perfect your treatment for the patient was. You can be upset about it, but don't internalize it and allow it to erode your confidence in your skills and abilities."

"You're good," Zora said to AJ. "You're like a therapist."

"We lawyers can be that, too. Didn't your mother tell you?" Zora and her mother chuckled. "That's better. At least I got you to laugh."

"Thank you."

"But your comment about feeling ambushed might be valid in this case," AJ said.

"My very thoughts," her mom said.

"Same," Silas said. "You know what? I sometimes play golf with Schyzman Senior. I can schedule one session with him tomorrow and see if I can gain some insights on his motivations for taking this case."

"That would be very helpful," AJ responded.

"Do you have the retainer agreement with you?" her mom said. "We can sign it now."

"Of course." He pulled up the briefcase he'd placed by the foot of his chair, extracted the documents, and handed them to Zora's mom. She read them, signed the retainer, and passed it to Zora to sign as well. Then her mom handed back the document plus an envelope Zora hadn't noticed to AJ. In less than a minute, they'd hired AJ for the job.

AJ then got to his feet. "I'll get started on this right away," he said. "My investigator is going to start with digging into the plaintiff's background. There might be something there that will help us."

"I'll have the documents ready for you tomorrow," Zora said.

"Perfect. Why don't we meet back here tomorrow at five p.m. to go through what we have so far?"

"Sounds good to me."

AJ stretched out his hand again to Zora. "I look forward to working with you."

Zora accepted his hand. "Likewise."

"Let me see you to the door," Zora's mom said. She got up and walked with him, and then they were out of sight.

"It's going to be alright," Silas says.

Zora ran a hand through her dark hair. "I hope so."

"It will. The case seems straightforward.

However, I'm more worried about the motivations behind it. Talking to Schyzman will be a step toward understanding that. I also think Dave shouldn't be involved in this. Right now, he should be staying under the radar. The cops have him in their sights, and we don't want this to create any additional problems for him."

"I'll talk to him tonight and stress the need to stay out of it," Zora promised.

"He'll buck against it, but it's really for the best." Zora's mom returned. "Alright, I need to get back to work."

"Thanks, Silas." Silas got up and headed back to the home office.

Zora stood, ready to carry back the tray she'd brought.

"Are you alright?" her mom asked.

Zora's hands stilled. She took a deep breath and let it out. "Not really, but what else can I do?" She picked up the tray. "I'm just going to hold tight, do the best I can, and pray everything works out fine."

"That's my girl!" Her mom followed her into the kitchen. "You know AJ likes you, right? I could see it as clear as day."

"Not interested." Zora placed the tray in the sink.

"I know. I told him that the door was closed. That you had a boyfriend."

She gave her mom a sharp look. "You talked about it?"

"I thought it might be fair for him to know up front, so he doesn't get his hopes up. But I said you could be friends if that was what you wanted."

"Okay, thanks."

Her mom reached out and gave her a hug. "Everything is going to work out. This, Dave's case, and anything else that might come up. You and Dave will be okay."

Zora hugged her back. She was planning on it, even though she didn't know how it'd happen.

Even though it seemed like things might get worse before they got better.

22

Zora arrived early to work the next day after tossing and turning all night. She'd tried to study some more when she'd realized trying to sleep was futile, but her mind had refused to focus on the books in front of her. The wrongful death lawsuit consumed her thoughts, and she couldn't understand why the plaintiffs wanted to file it, no matter how much she tried to reason it out.

Everything she'd done had been by the book and experience, and her colleagues had agreed so too. So why? Was it the anguish they felt from losing a loved one, or was there more at play here? After all Zora had been through, she couldn't rule out the latter option.

Zora didn't know what it was about her that drew

them like moths to a flame, but she seemed to be a magnet for all kinds of trouble. They somehow ended up on her plate, even when she did her best to avoid them. Was there something written on her forehead that marked her out as easy prey? Because she hadn't done anything beyond her call of duty to give the best care she could to patients. Was it now so wrong to be compassionate and caring to those who trusted her that her own life had to be at risk?

A part of her wanted to run away from it all. It was hard dealing with all the heartache, stress, and threats in her life. Lexinbridge was supposed to be a safe city, yet it seemed to have more than its fair share of crime and corruption in its underbelly. But was there any other city out there that was truly safe? Besides, Zora loved this city and couldn't imagine living anywhere else. But that didn't mean she enjoyed having to deal with yet another career-threatening situation.

She changed from the scrubs she'd worn for her morning round into a cream blouse paired with a pair of black slacks as her mind continued to dwell on the case. Now if there was more at play, then she needed to protect herself, which included getting her hands on evidence that wouldn't disappear. The hospital did its best to protect its information, but it was better to be safe than sorry.

Zora pulled up to a workstation in the residents' on-call room, signed in, and downloaded a copy of her intake notes, surgical notes, preliminary autopsy diagnoses she'd received via email from the pathologist, and the residents' handbook onto a USB drive.

Then she remembered the discrepancy between the scan report and what she'd seen when she'd opened the patient. Even though there was a likelihood that was normal, Zora didn't think that was the case here. So she transferred a copy of the scan report to a system folder for her own records. Then she logged out, returned the USB drive to the bag in her locker, pulled on her medical coat, and left the resident lounge. Zora then headed to the elevators and five minutes later, was on her way into the clinic.

So far, no one at work had mentioned anything about the malpractice suit—it seemed those who knew about it were keeping it under wraps, which suited Zora just fine. She prayed it would remain that way.

Patients already filled the clinic's waiting area when Zora arrived, and she suspected the clinic would run long—there were likely more patients on their way. Then she spotted the last person she wanted to see. Why was he in today's clinic and not in the one later this week? Hopefully, he'd just stay in his own lane and ignore her.

"Well, well, well, look who the cat dragged in. Zora Smyth," Herbert boomed.

Her shoulders tightened. Why couldn't he just pretend he didn't see her? She noticed some patients staring at her.

Zora hid her disdain for Herbert and forced a smile onto her face. "Hello, Herbert." He'd just disrespected her, but she wasn't going to lower herself to his level. It was best to keep walking and ignore him. She made her way through the waiting area toward where the clinic's offices were.

"Why are you here?" he continued in the same volume. "Shouldn't you be at home taking care of your wrongful death lawsuit, the one they're serving you with because you killed a patient?"

The patients around her gasped, and Zora's breath hitched. He must have heard about the lawsuit from his connection at the hospital. How dare he embarrass her here in front of their patients! The attending would have reprimanded him, but Zora doubted he'd arrived. That's why Herbert had been bold enough to do it.

Coward. There was no point responding to him;

doing so would just be belittling herself. So even though his words hurt like physical lashes on her body and she felt the pitying glances from the nurses and medical staff, Zora forced herself to keep walking. Soon she reached her assigned office, entered, and shut the door behind her. Then she spent the next few minutes calming herself down in readiness for the clinic.

Five minutes later, the clinic began. Zora saw some old and a few new patients. After a while, she waited for the next patient to come in, but none did.

That's strange. She looked at her watch and frowned. It was too early for the clinic to slow down, considering how many patients had been in the waiting area. She got up, poked her head out of the office, and hailed a passing nurse. "Are all the patients gone for the day?" she asked.

"No." The nurse couldn't look her in the eye.

"So why haven't I gotten the next patient?"

"Dr. Smyth… the rest of the patients you were supposed to see have switched over to the other doctors. We tried to convince them, but they insisted."

Her heart sank. It had to be because of what Herbert had said. "Thank you."

The nurse nodded and left.

Zora leaned against the frame of her door. As much as it hurt, she couldn't let it get to her. She had no choice but to make the most of the situation. There was no point in staying if she couldn't see any patients. So she stepped out, knocked on the door of the attending's office, and poked her head in. He was busy with a patient, so she just gestured that she had to leave, and he nodded in understanding.

Zora shut his door, squared her shoulders, and walked out of the clinic with confidence. She'd done nothing wrong and had no reason to hide. If the clinic didn't need her, then her time was better spent prepping for the exams before she had her afternoon round.

Zora entered her family home. Her legal team—AJ, Silas, and her mom—were already waiting for her at the dining table.

She settled into the seat next to her mom and dropped her satchel beside her. "Hello, everyone. Sorry, I'm late," she said. "There was a last-minute emergency with a patient."

"No worries," AJ said, flashing her a smile. "We

were just getting started. Silas, why don't you go first?"

Silas leaned back, his tie nowhere near his neck. Zora hid a smile. It seemed dating her mom was loosening him up. "The Schyzmans are nutcases," he said. "They made this big deal about being too busy and having no time to the point of being rude. It was quite embarrassing."

"I'm so sorry, dear." Zora's mom squeezed his hand on the table.

"Oh, I wasn't embarrassed. I was mortified *for them*." AJ and Zora chuckled. "You should have seen the looks they received after that. They were the talk of the day." Then his eyes twinkled. "But I learned something when I popped in to use the men's room. They didn't realize anyone was still there. I didn't hear their earlier words, but Schyzman Senior was warning Junior to keep his mouth shut and not talk about the Smyth case, since they'd already been paid. He even said the walls had ears, which was actually true in this case!" Everyone chuckled, including Zora.

"Paying the lawyer up front isn't the norm in wrongful death suits from what I know and could either mean they're one hundred percent sure they'll win the case, or they have another motive," her mom said.

"Or the client can more than afford it," Zora interjected.

AJ shook his head. "Not in this case. We discovered the deceased is from a very low-income family—he was the one supporting his mother."

"So the money must be coming from somewhere else," Zora said.

"Exactly."

"But from who? And why?"

"That's what we need to find out," AJ said. "But that's not all."

"What else?" Zora asked.

"I found out the deceased was a twin."

"Twin?" her mom said.

"Identical," AJ clarified. "And he's missing."

"Since when?" Zora asked.

"Since Friday evening," AJ replied.

"Have they filed a missing person's report?" Silas asked.

"Not yet. Maybe they believe he's not missing and will show up soon."

"But it's too much of a coincidence for us to overlook it," Zora said.

"Exactly," AJ said. "We even heard they're inseparable, so why is he not around to support his family? It's just odd, so we plan to keep digging."

"Speaking of, that reminds me of something I'm not sure I've mentioned yet," Zora said.

All eyes turned to her. "What is it?" AJ asked.

"One thing that stuck out to me in the OR after we opened him up was that the CT scan had shown that his splenic capsule, the lining that covers the spleen, was intact. But when we opened him up, I found a large laceration on the splenic surface. That's something that should have been evident on the CT scan. But the patient went into anaphylaxis at that point, so all our focus shifted to saving his life."

AJ rubbed his dimpled chin. "So you're thinking there's foul play involved?"

"Honestly, I don't know," Zora replied. "But it's been bugging me."

AJ leaned back. "Okay, I have a theory, but I'm going to dig some more to get evidence that supports it before I share what it is."

"Alright." Zora dug into her satchel and extracted the USB drive. "And here's the information you requested." She extended it to AJ.

"Thank you. I'm sure this will be very helpful." He tucked it into his briefcase.

"So what's next?" Zora asked.

"You let us work our magic. We'll follow up with the brother to see what we can find. My team is already pulling together materials for the case and identifying expert witnesses. We've also started prepping for the pre-suit negotiations, even though Zora has stated she won't settle. We'll also try to trace the source of the money behind the lawsuit."

"Let me take care of that," Zora's mom said. "My team is good at this."

"That would be great. We'll also let you know if we come across any clues that might help with that as we search for the brother."

"Perfect," her mom said.

Then AJ turned to Zora and gave her a small smile. "And Dr. Smyth, keep staying calm. I know it's hard to do, but you're already doing a great job of it. Keep up the good work." Then he turned back to everyone. "Thank you," he said.

"AJ, can I speak with you for a minute?" Silas said. "I have a question about personal injury claims regarding a criminal case I have."

"Sure." AJ got up and walked with Silas until they were out of earshot.

"Mom, where's Alisa?" Zora asked, as she stretched her legs beneath the table.

"She's still in the office. Why?"

"Just asking. What about Dave?"

"He went out. He was going stir crazy and needed to take care of some business." Her mom lowered her voice. "He received some death threats—he hid the messages, but I saw them all the same. And then he got a call from his landlord that someone had vandalized his place. So, I had to let him leave. But he said he'll be back tonight." Seeing the panic on Zora's face, "He took the news pretty well, and I'm sure he'll be fine. Don't worry. I even put a security detail on him to make sure he stays safe."

Zora hoped that was the case, because she wasn't sure how she'd survive if anything happened to Dave.

23

Dave waited in the shadows and watched as two security guards—one younger and the other much older—exited the brick guardhouse that secured the nursing home on the city's outskirts. The younger guard said a few words to the older one and then turned and passed through the gates before swaggering down the driveway that led through well-manicured lawns to the main entrance of the nursing home. The older guard glanced around and then went back inside the guardhouse.

Thank goodness he'd ditched the security tail that Zora's mom had put on him after he'd left his apartment. He'd met the landlord, and the cost to repair the apartment had been minimal. Dave had agreed to foot the bill. It had been fine having the tail on him throughout that time. But now Dave wanted no witnesses for what he was about to do.

He waited a minute, then strode toward the guardhouse and knocked on the door. The door swung open, and the older guard stared at him, surprise written all over his face. "Come in," he said. "I sensed someone was watching me."

Dave followed him into the room. The space was bland but neat, with security monitors showing footage of different parts of the property. "Good to see you again, Old Sam," he said. Old Sam was an ex-cop that had retired a few years ago. Dave had covered for Old Sam when he'd had to keep missing work so close to his retirement because his daughter had been very sick. Eventually, Old Sam had retired and had received his pension with no issues. Now he worked evenings at the nursing home for some extra cash.

"Would you like some coffee?" Old Sam asked. He offered Dave some from the flask he'd picked up from the table.

"No, thank you," Dave said. "I have a question for you, though."

Old Sam sipped from the cup he'd poured for

himself. "I didn't believe it one bit when I heard about what they said you did."

"What's the word on the street?" Dave asked. Old Sam had always had his ear to the ground, and that hadn't changed now that he was retired.

Old Sam stayed silent while he took another sip of his coffee. "I heard there's a bounty on your head."

A bounty? Someone meant business. "Who put out the bounty?"

Sam shook his head. "I don't know. But the bounty is for a million dollars."

Dave's heart skipped a beat. That was a lot of money. It had to be someone he'd really ticked off, and it narrowed the possibilities.

Old Sam set the cup on the table. "I think it's time you left. My partner may be on his way back, and the last thing I need is for him to see you here and start asking questions."

"Okay. Thanks."

"Just be careful and lie low until this blows over, okay?"

"I will." There was no more to be said.

Dave turned and left the place.

———

Old Sam watched Dave leave and then settled back into his chair while he poured another cup of coffee for himself. Then he pulled a burner phone from his pant pocket and made a call.

The call connected after one ring. "He just left," Old Sam said to the person on the other end of the line. Then the line went dead.

He tucked the phone back into his pocket and closed his eyes. Guilt riddled his heart at what he'd just done.

But he had no choice.

Old Sam had to save his daughter from the monsters that threatened her.

Dave stepped out of the train he'd taken into the city from its outskirts, the smell of brake shoes and coffee beans—from a nearby coffee stand—assaulting his nostrils. He pulled his cap lower and wove his way through the crowd at the busy train station. Folks scurried off in different directions like busy ants off to do their duty. Soon he reached the flight of stairs he'd been looking for and headed up them toward the street level.

Then he noticed the thugs blocking the exit.

These young men in their twenties wore black T-shirts under their starter jackets, sagging pants, and baseball caps tilted at an angle. A few sported red bandanas instead. Their jackets had gang symbols or graffiti written on them, and most wore gaudy neck chains or earrings. Dave was pretty sure they'd weapons hidden on their persons.

What were they doing out here in the open, instead of gathering in dark areas to avoid being seen? But this was not the time to mess with them. Dave turned to go back down and use another exit, only to find a second set of thugs behind him.

They'd boxed him in.

Dave sighed. It seemed the news about the bounty on his head had spread, and this gang was looking to collect on it. But how had they found him? He'd had no tail before and after he'd joined the train—Dave had checked to make sure.

He rolled his shoulders. Those were questions he'd find answers to once he'd dealt with the situation at hand without getting locked up in jail.

Dave had to beat them at their own game, or die trying.

Zora and her mom were just about to send AJ off when her mom's phone rang.

Her mom answered the call. "What is it?" she said. Zora watched as her mom's face lost color.

Zora's heart beat faster. "What's going on?" she asked.

"Okay. Thanks," her mom said to the person on the other end of the line. She ended the call.

Then her mom locked eyes with Zora. "It's Dave. He's in the hospital."

Alisa paced through her office, her bare feet sinking into the plush carpet.

What was going on? She'd been too nervous to wait until Friday and had called Charles. Instead, the number had rung through as it had on subsequent attempts. Charles hadn't returned her calls. She hadn't been able to reach Pete either, who was now in Africa, to see if he'd heard anything about him.

The only option left was to go to Charles' office and look for him. But she was in the middle of a big case for a major client, and her team was working late into the evenings. Even lunch and dinner were being delivered for them. Alisa didn't want to visit

Crescent Street after dark, so going there was off the table for now.

She slumped into her swivel chair. Had Charles disappeared? Had he only been stringing her along? But why would he do that? Alisa couldn't think of any reason for it. Right now, her best bet was to wait a few more days till her current client's work was done, and then she'd hunt him down.

Her phone rang. Maybe it was Charles.

Alisa scrambled across her desk to pick it up, only to see her mom's number flashing on the screen.

Her shoulders fell. She'd gotten all excited, but it was her own fault—Charles couldn't have called her on this number since he didn't have it.

Alisa swiped the answer button. "Hello, Mom."

"Are you done for the day?" her mom asked.

"Yes. I'm just about to leave the office."

"We just got to Lexinbridge Regional. Dave is in the hospital."

Interesting. Maybe she could gather some clues from Dave himself. He might spill a few secrets while he was loopy from whatever drug cocktail they'd given him. This was a chance she couldn't pass up. "I'll be right there," she said and ended the call.

Alisa sprang up from her chair. It was time to hurry while she still had the opportunity.

Zora burst into Dave's hospital room and came to a halt a few feet away from the side of the bed. Dave was awake with his head in a swath of bandages. He sat up slowly and gave Zora a small smile as she approached. He had bruises all over the exposed parts of his body, and his left eye was swollen. An IV line snaked from its stand into his forearm.

Zora didn't know whether to kiss him for being alive or strangle him for his stubbornness. She reached him and gave him a light hug, though she could tell from his movements that it hurt a little.

"I'm sorry," Dave said.

"I can't have anything happen to you too," Zora said, even as her voice broke. Dave kissed her forehead and held her close like he knew what she'd not said—like it had happened to Marcus. She still missed Marcus, though it had been a couple of months since he'd died.

Then Zora released him. "How are you feeling?" she asked softly.

He gave her a lopsided grin, and the dimples she loved so much made their appearance. "Everything hurts, but not too bad. No major organs were harmed in the process." She caught his hand in hers and held it. "Don't forget the security guy—he fought just as hard," Dave said.

Zora nodded. "He's in the next room. I'll drop by and see him once I'm done here."

Zora's mom stepped forward. "Dave, I'm glad you're okay." Zora hadn't noticed when she'd entered. "We heard what happened. Silas sends his greetings." Silas had had to go back to the office.

"Thank you, ma'am," Dave responded.

"You'll take my advice next time, right?"

Dave gave her mom a sheepish grin. Then the smile faded as he stared at something behind her.

Zora followed his gaze, only to see AJ standing nearby. "Oh, that's my lawyer, AJ Beckett. We just finished a meeting when the call about you came through, so he came along. AJ, meet Detective Dave McKesson, my boyfriend."

"Nice to meet you, Detective," AJ said.

Dave considered him for a moment and then responded. "Same here. Thanks for helping Zora."

Zora rolled her eyes. Guys! Always marking their territory. She guessed Dave would bring this up later.

A phone vibrated, and AJ pulled his phone from his jacket. "Hello." He listened for a few minutes and then said, "I'll be there shortly." He tucked his phone back into his pocket. Then he turned to Zora. "I'll see you later, Zora, ma'am," he said.

He'd never called her Zora. Probably did it to rile up Dave, and it seemed to work from the questioning look Dave gave her. That discussion was definitely going to happen.

"Good night, AJ," Zora said. "Thanks for coming with us."

"I'll see myself out," AJ said. He walked away and left the room.

Zora turned back to Dave. "Let me help you lie down." Dave let out a happy sigh when he was more comfortable.

The door to the hospital room burst open, and Alisa hurried in.

Zora's eyes widened. What was Alisa doing here?

"You need to see this." Alisa grabbed the remote from the nightstand and switched on the TV.

———

"What's going on?" Zora asked Alisa.

"Hold on one second," Alisa said. "I just saw this on my way in." Soon, she found the channel she was seeking. It was a female reporter giving the news update for the hour. Then the screen flashed to some lawyers behind a podium, addressing the press.

"Wait! Isn't that Schyzman?" her mother pointed to an older man with white hair and bushy eyebrows.

"The lawyer?" Zora's heart beat faster. This couldn't be good.

Her mom pulled her phone from her pocket and speed-dialed a number. "Silas, you need to put on the TV. It's Schyzman." She ended the call.

Zora watched with trepidation and then horror as Schyzman stated that they'd filed a lawsuit against a certain Dr. Zora Smyth on behalf of their client. They'd learned Dr. Smyth had been under the influence of drugs while operating on the patient, who'd then died in her care.

Zora heard nothing else. Schyzman had just struck what sounded like a death knell to her career and dreams. She'd been this close, just a few more weeks to making it. With this news about Zora operating under the influence, which was false by the way, the hospital could fire her, the state medical licensing board could suspend her license to practice, she'd never get a chance to finish her residency anywhere in the country let alone take the board exams, and her years and years of sacrifice to become a surgeon would be all for nothing.

Sounds faded in and out, and she shook her head to clear it. This shouldn't be happening. *This shouldn't be happening!*

Then her mother's voice pierced the bubble around her ears. "How dare he? How dare he?" she said, her voice rising higher and higher as she spoke.

"Mom, calm down," Alisa said.

"Calm down? This pompous fool wants to ruin my daughter's life, and you want me to calm down? But he just made a big mistake. He just poked the hornet's nest, and he's definitely going to get bitten. He doesn't know who he's dealing with."

She turned to Zora and gripped her shoulders. "Listen to me, baby girl. I'm going to take care of this idiot. Trust me. You know I can do it, right?" Zora nodded. "Good. I need you to hang in there. Let

Mama Bear take care of it. Can you do that for me?" Zora nodded again. "Good."

Her mom hailed a member of the security detail that had followed them to the hospital. "Take care of Dr. Smyth and make sure she gets home safely. Don't let her leave your sight."

"Yes, ma'am," the young man said.

"Dave, we'll talk later. Alisa, let's go." Zora's mom strode out of the room.

"Where are we going?" Alisa asked as she hurried after her. Alisa kept looking back at Dave, as if she had something to say to him. *Weird*, Zora thought.

"To prepare for war."

"Clive, you said you found something?" AJ said to the man in the green windbreaker who was leaning against one of the hospital pillars. AJ had gotten his call and hurried from Zora's side to meet him.

"I'm hungry. Feed me first," Clive said.

AJ chuckled as he looked around. Then he noticed a café with a cute blue-and-white-striped awning across the street. It had the open sign visible on its door. "Let's grab something there."

A few minutes later, they sat by the window with Clive digging into a plate of barbecue chicken sliders. AJ had ordered the same, and it was delicious. They focused on the food for a while, and then Clive leaned back. "This was so worth coming here to look for you," he said.

"Now I know what food to order if I'm ever in this area again." AJ took a sip from his glass of water and then leaned back. "Okay, tell me what you found."

"I went to look for the deceased's twin at his usual haunts. His name is Xavier Young, by the way. No one had seen him. I struck gold at the fifth place I went to. A friend of his had seen Oliver on Saturday afternoon, sometime around eight p.m. He'd been injured."

"Wait! What do you mean Oliver? He's the deceased one, right?"

"I had the same reaction. So I asked the guy why he was so sure it was Oliver. He said Oliver has a mole on his left shoulder, and Xavier doesn't. Oliver was shirtless when he saw him."

"How's he sure it was on a Saturday and not a Friday?"

"He said he was on his way to band practice with a group of friends, and that only happens over the weekend since he has work all week."

"Oh, my goodness. This is getting interesting."

"I couldn't believe my ears either," Clive said.

"So on what part of his body was Oliver injured?"

"Right here." Clive pointed to the upper part of the left stomach.

AJ's pulse quickened. "That's the same area of the body where he—I mean, his dead brother in the morgue had the stab wound."

"Exactly. What are the odds of that? The friend said when he stepped into the room and announced his presence, Oliver had covered it up so fast, like he had his pants on fire."

AJ raised his eyebrow. "He really said that? Pants on fire?"

Clive grinned. "Well, I paraphrased."

AJ chuckled. "Anything else?"

"That's it."

"So, what do you think?" AJ asked.

"Those brothers had something cooking up between them, and it wasn't ramen. Definitely something they didn't want anyone to know about."

"So Oliver is alive. We have to find him," AJ said.

"I agree. Already sent out feelers to track him down. I also have someone following the mother, just in case she knows something."

"We may also need to do a DNA test to make sure it's him, but I don't know how that works with identical twins."

"Why don't you ask Dr. Smyth? She'll know more."

"You're right." AJ pulled out his phone and dialed her number. She answered after a few rings. "Hello, Dr. Smyth. Do you think you could spare a few minutes and come down to the café across from the hospital? It's about the case."

"O-okay. Give me a few minutes," Zora said from the other end of the line.

"Alright, thanks." He ended the call. "She's on her way," he said to Clive.

"You're sweet on her."

AJ fought to keep his face passive, but he could feel his ears warming up. "Why do you say that? She's just our client."

"Your voice. I only hear that voice come to play when you're speaking to a lady you like."

AJ took a sip of his water. "Be serious, Clive."

Clive raised his hands in surrender. "If you say so. But I call it like I see it. And that's the gospel truth from a man who's married to his sweetheart of twenty years and has four daughters."

"Just make sure you don't mention this when Dr. Smyth gets here. This is a strictly business relationship, and she has a boyfriend."

Clive cocked an eyebrow. "You already found that out?"

"Oh, buzz off."

Clive chuckled and took another sip of his water.

The bell above the café's entrance jingled. AJ turned to see Dr. Smyth walk into the café, her dark, wavy hair bouncing in a ponytail behind her. She looked different, but he couldn't tell why. She noticed him and headed in their direction. A young man came in after her but sat down at a nearby table. AJ and Clive stood up as she approached.

"Hello, AJ," she said. "I thought you'd be home by now."

"I would be, if not for him." He pointed to Clive. "Meet Clive Munroe, investigator extraordinaire, and lead investigator at our law firm."

"It's nice to meet you." Zora extended her hand for a shake.

"Nice to meet you too, Doctor," Clive said.

"Oh, please call me Zora." AJ could tell from the pleased smile on Clive's face he liked her immediately.

"Shall we?" AJ motioned to the empty seat beside him. Zora sat down. "Do you want anything?"

"A cup of coffee. Black."

"Coming right up." He motioned to a nearby waiter and gave him the order.

"Is it me, or is that man two tables away watching us?" Clive said.

"That's my security detail," Zora responded.

The waiter returned with the coffee.

"Thank you," Zora said.

The waiter acknowledged it with a nod and left.

"Is everything alright?" AJ asked.

Zora dismissed the concern. "Just a precautionary measure. So, what's going on, AJ?"

"Well, it turns out Oliver might be alive."

Zora stared at him in surprise. "Are you playing tricks on me, AJ? It's not funny."

"This isn't a joke. His twin brother, Xavier, might be the one lying in the morgue." AJ recounted everything Clive had just told him.

Zora leaned back. "Unbelievable. So this might be a setup."

"My very thoughts," Clive said.

"But why?"

"We won't know until we find Oliver," AJ said. "We also need to do a DNA test to prove Xavier is the one in the morgue."

"That might not work since they're identical twins," Zora responded. "DNA tests to differentiate twins are new and evolving and currently can't hold up in any legal courts. Only good old fingerprinting and dental records can differentiate identical twins for now. We can get a set from the body in the morgue, but what can we compare it to?"

"Unless either of them has one of those jobs that require fingerprinting like a daycare worker, has a criminal record, or owns a gun permit, their fingerprints might not be in the system," Clive said. "I've checked, and they don't have criminal records."

"And I doubt they've been in the military, which makes it difficult unless we find Oliver," AJ said.

"But he could still claim he is Xavier," Zora said.

"True," Clive said. "But then he has the mole."

"Which he can easily remove. Having a scar in the same spot is not the same thing, and I doubt the mole evidence alone would hold up in court."

"So we'll look into the dental records and see if they have those," Clive said.

"Yes, dental records would work, since their names would already be on them," AJ said. "But it doesn't hurt to find Oliver, too. Just having him present, as well as having the wound on the same site, is enough to cast suspicion on the case."

"Agreed," Clive said. "We'll keep looking for him."

"So if Xavier was the one who died, who arrived at the ER? Oliver or Xavier?" Zora asked.

"My guess would be Oliver, though we don't have proof of that," AJ said.

"So if it was Oliver who came to the ER, and Xavier who died in the OR, when did the switch happen?" Clive asked.

"The elevators!" Zora and AJ said together.

"What are you talking about?" Clive asked, looking from Zora to AJ.

"The patient arrived later than I expected to the OR, and my resident, who was supposed to be with the patient until he got to the OR, said that the surgical elevators were delayed," Zora replied.

"But that doesn't matter as long as your resident was with him," Clive noted.

AJ leaned forward. "Unless he wasn't. What if he stepped away from the patient, even if it was for a brief moment?"

Zora pulled her phone out and dialed a number. "Dr. Johnson, this is Dr. Smyth," Zora said. "I have a question for you about the table death patient. Was there any time you stepped away from him while you guys were bringing him to the OR?" Zora listened to his response. "Really? Not even for two minutes? You won't be penalized in any way. I just need you to tell me the truth." Zora listened some more. "Okay. Thank you very much." She ended the call.

"What did he say?" AJ asked.

"While the elevators were delayed, he had to go use the men's room. But get this: the orderlies were the ones who encouraged him to do so. So he went for like two minutes and came back."

"That was enough time for the switch to have happened," Clive said.

"Yes, more than enough time. But how did they know he'd need to use the bathroom?" AJ said.

"One of them had offered him a bottle of water while he'd waited for the shift handover to finish. That was the first delay before the second one by the elevators," Zora said.

"So someone could have slipped him something, and he would have been none the wiser," Clive said.

"Exactly, but we can't prove that now. That evidence would be long gone," AJ said.

"But there's CCTV," Zora said.

"Bingo," Clive said.

"There's one near that set of elevators," Zora continued. "I've noticed it a couple of times when taking patients up to the OR. I don't think there's any in the ER where the shift handover took place because of patient privacy concerns."

"So let's add the CCTV footage to our list, shall we?" AJ said.

"Done," Clive said. "We'll also need to look into those orderlies."

"It might be harder for you to get the CCTV since it's from a hospital," Zora commented.

Clive winked. "We have our ways." Zora laughed.

"Nice to see you laugh," AJ said. "I was wondering if everything was alright."

"Just a little overwhelming," Zora said. "But I'll be fine." Her phone buzzed, and she looked at the screen.

AJ noticed her frown. "Is everything okay?" he asked.

"The hospital committee wants to see me tomorrow. I'm sure it's about the case. They probably saw the news."

"What news?" AJ asked.

"The one where Schyzman claimed that I was on drugs when I operated on the patient."

AJ's anger rose at what Schyzman had done. "That's ridiculous!" He made a mental note to ask Clive to hunt down the news recording later.

Zora smiled wearily. "I know."

"I'm so sorry," Clive said.

"Are you okay?" AJ asked.

"I'm fine," Zora said.

"Well, you need your lawyer to go with you to that meeting," AJ said. "Would it be okay if I came with you?"

"Could you? I also want Silas there, since he's familiar with them."

"What time tomorrow?" AJ asked.

"Ten a.m."

"That works for me. I'll call you when I get there."

"Thanks, AJ. Listen, I have to go. It was nice meeting you, Clive. I hope we meet again under better circumstances."

"Me too. Take care of yourself, Doctor." At Zora's raised eyebrow: "Zora, I mean."

Zora rose to her feet. "Have a good night, gentlemen." She turned and left the café, her security detail trailing behind her.

"Such a nice lady," Clive said. "I hope everything works out for her."

"Me too, Clive. Me too," AJ said.

It was what he prayed for.

And he hoped it would begin with the meeting tomorrow.

J amie Tanner had always dreamed of the finer things of life and had planned to study hard to get admitted into college on scholarship, but growing up with an alcoholic mother and an abusive father had gotten him out of the house and on his own before he'd finished high school. He'd dropped out to work at the local grocery store where they'd paid him minimum wage, which did little for his bank account.

But Jamie couldn't let go of his dream. He studied hard and passed his GED and then applied for a spot in the pharmacy technician program at his local community college. He'd only chosen the program because a girl who looked like his ideal dream date had told him she was applying to the program as well. Jamie earned the certificate after a year, and through the connections of the grocery store manager, had gotten a job at a local retail pharmacy. The pay was much better, and Jamie could move into a studio apartment of his own. He was moving up in the world.

Over the next few years, Jamie's pay only got marginally better, and he worried his dream would never come true.

Then one day, his luck changed. A sharp-looking man, dressed to the nines, stopped by at Jamie's table at a local café where he was having lunch. The man painted a pretty picture of how Jamie could make so much wealth that Jamie felt his dreams stirring to life again. All he had to do was short some dispensed medications a little here or there, adjust the inventory shipment just a little, and not verify a few random prescriptions. It was up to Jamie how he wanted it.

At first, Jamie resisted. How could he do such a thing? But then he watched his colleagues and saw some were already ahead of the game. Doing the same wouldn't matter, right?

So Jamie joined the racket, and soon his wealth ballooned. He was careful not to do too much and kept spreading his wealth around. Eventually, Jamie started living the life he wanted.

He bought a car and then a house, claiming the money was from some inheritance. He married a girl he met at a local speed-dating event, Mary, and then they had two girls. Life was good, and Jamie wanted it to stay so.

He moved pharmacies about every three years so as not to arouse suspicion. He got promoted over the years until he became a chief pharmacy technician and then landed the job as the head pharmacy technician for Lexinbridge Regional Hospital's pain clinic.

That was when the mega bucks rolled in. Jamie opened offshore accounts, kept a much simpler life at home, but lived large whenever he travelled on vacation. His family enjoyed the times abroad with him and never questioned where the money came from.

Then a week ago, Jamie got a visit that changed his life again. A new man, the one with mean eyes, told him he could choose to surrender himself to the cops, get a smart lawyer, serve a minimum sentence, and then live the rest of his life outside the country, enjoying the enormous wealth he'd accumulated, or get his throat and the throats of his family slit at night in their beds.

Jamie was a smart man who knew how to roll his dice. His dream had to stay alive.

So he walked up the steps of the police station that Tuesday night and turned himself in.

Zora stepped into the conference room and settled into the middle chair on the empty side of the conference table. Silas and AJ took the seats on her left and right. The hospital committee, made up of three men and a lady, already sat on the other side of the table. Zora noted the hospital's legal counsel, Tim Gardner, was also present with his associate.

"Good morning," Zora said. The committee members mumbled their greetings in return. She could tell from their facial expressions they'd rather be anywhere else but in the room.

"Why don't we get started?" Tim said after Zora had introduced Silas and AJ. He leveled his gaze on Zora. "So, Dr. Smyth, there has been allegations against you that you were under the influence when you operated on the deceased patient, a Mr. Oliver Young."

"Allegations which are false," Silas countered. Zora's team had agreed she wouldn't speak unless Silas gave her the go-ahead.

"That's what you say," a bespectacled member of the committee replied.

"Dr. Smyth is innocent of any charges unless proven otherwise," Silas said.

The lady member leaned forward. "And that's why we want her to take a drug test," she said.

"I don't see why she wouldn't want to take it to clear her name," a red-haired committee member concurred.

Sure, it was easy to go along with their request, but what if the results got tainted in the process? It wasn't above whoever was manipulating everything behind the scenes to do so, and once the results were out, Zora's team wouldn't be able to turn back the clock, and Zora would be stuck with a damning evidence. No way was she going to shoot herself in the foot.

Silas leaned forward. "This so-called charge against Dr. Smyth does not qualify under the pre-employment, reasonable suspicion, or post-accident situations in which the hospital can request a drug test from her. Dr. Smyth has never demonstrated any signs or symptoms of working under the influence, and there are no witnesses or evidence to corroborate the accusation. So asking her to take a drug test would be contravening federal and state laws for workplace protection for employees, which, I can assure you, would invite a lawsuit against the hospital."

"Unless we get a warrant," Tim said.

"Good luck with that," Silas countered.

By now, Zora could see that some members of the committee were annoyed, while others maintained stoic facial expressions—Zora couldn't guess what they were thinking. The lady member conferred with the lawyer and then turned back to Zora. "Is there anything else you'd like to say before we ask you to step out for a few minutes while we discuss and come back with our recommendation?" she said.

AJ opened his briefcase and retrieved a USB drive. "Just a little matter we want to clear up," he said. He extended the device to Tim.

"What's this?" Tim asked.

"Just some important evidence you need to look at about this case," AJ said.

Tim considered AJ for a moment, then accepted

the USB drive. He handed it over to his associate, who had been recording the meeting notes.

The associate plugged it into his laptop, which he then hooked up to the overhead projector. He pressed a button on a remote on the table, and a screen descended near one wall. Soon, an image filled the screen.

The committee members watched with indifference and then horror as they recognized the bank of elevators on the screen and the activity that was playing out on the footage.

The bespectacled member jumped to his feet. "How did you get this?" he bellowed as he pointed an accusing finger at AJ. "This is illegal!"

Zora could see Tim already making a call, probably to the hospital's security office, to explain how an external party had gotten hold of its CCTV footage.

"Please calm down," AJ said. "As you can see, they switched out a certain patient heading up with another individual. Said patient is the Mr. Oliver Young who is supposed to be dead and lying in the morgue. So you can see why my client is concerned about this."

Tim finished his call and jumped back into the foray. "Dr. Smyth, getting a copy of our security footage is a serious issue against you," he said in a stern voice.

Silas leaned back and steepled his fingers. "I'd like to remind you that a patient switch, like what we've witnessed on the screen, is a more serious security breach, and has dire consequences for the hospital if the news gets out," he said. "Maybe it might be in your best interest to launch a thorough investigation before pointing fingers?"

But AJ wasn't done. "Oh, and by the way, we've already identified the two orderlies in this video," he said. "We have their sworn testimonies they were ordered to look the other way while the patient was being switched, or their families would come to harm."

"Unbelievable!" the red-haired member said. Zora could see the other committee members were agitated as well.

Her shoulders relaxed, and she exhaled. It seemed her team's strategy was working.

Now the ball was in the hospital's court, and Zora had a fair idea how the rest of the discussion would shake out.

Zora stepped out of the conference room with Silas and AJ in tow. She'd held onto the small hope things would turn around, and it had pulled through for her.

They'd gotten the hospital to back off.

Of course, Zora and AJ still had to find the living twin and prove he was the real Oliver Young. Still, it had worked out well, and Zora felt lighter than before. But she was tired and exhausted and now planned to rest for the remainder of the day.

"So how's my mom?" Zora asked Silas as they waited for the elevator to arrive. "I don't think she spent the night at home, and I didn't see her this morning before I left."

Silas chuckled. "Your mom just started a war and is having a glorious time suing Schyzman and Schyzman front, back, and center. She knows a lot of their secrets and is determined to sink that firm. The partners have been running around like headless chickens, having meetings behind closed doors to decide what to do. Even though the firm belongs to Schyzman Senior, the collective shares of the equity partners are greater than his and his son's, so they can overrule him in dire circumstances."

"Like this," Zora said.

"Right."

Silas' phone vibrated, and he pulled it out. He

tapped the screen to read the message and then chuckled. "The partners of Schyzman and Schyzman have approached your mom. They've offered to retract their statement, issue a public apology to Zora, and pay for damages. Apparently, a client with deep pockets paid Schyzman to ruin and disgrace Zora."

"That's the way to do it," AJ said with a fist pump in the air. He noticed some medical staff looking at him strangely, so he straightened his frame and adjusted his collar.

Zora chuckled. He was such a dork.

The elevator doors opened, and they stepped in. Soon they reached the ground floor.

As they exited the elevator, Silas' phone vibrated again. He looked at the screen and answered the call. "Hello." As he listened, his eyes turned on Zora and held her gaze. Then he ended the call.

"Zora, we need to get you home NOW!" he said.

The security detail that had waited for Zora and her team at the hospital's entrance snuck Zora and Silas into the house through the hidden back door—a squad car that had come to pick Zora up for questioning had blocked the front gate's entrance. AJ had returned to his office.

"Zora, thank goodness you're home," her mom said as she wrapped her into a hug.

"Mom, what's going on?"

"Remember Dave's case?" Zora nodded. "The cops found prescription drugs in that cache besides the heroin. A witness has come forward to say that you supplied him with the signed prescription pads that were used to order those drugs in exchange for opioid analgesics."

"What?" Zora said.

"Does anyone still use prescription pads in this day and age?" Silas asked.

"We rarely use them, except when the system is down, which happened recently." A lightbulb went off in Zora's head. "That may be when this Jamie fellow took a copy of my pad and forged the signature! I don't sign the pad until I've written the prescription, so you'll never find a blank pad with my actual signature on it."

"Good girl," her mom said.

"Shouldn't it be easy to prove it's not her handwriting?" Silas asked.

"It should, except that the cops got hold of a copy of Zora's signature and compared it to that on the pad, and it's a match," her mom said.

"That's a fake analysis," Zora said. "We just need a better handwriting expert to counteract it."

"The issue is that it takes time, and time is the one thing we don't have," her mom said. "I don't think that squad car is going to leave until they bring a warrant and have you down at the station."

"I'm not going," Zora said. She'd done nothing wrong, and she was sick and tired of the bad guys and the cops pushing her to the wall when all she wanted to do was focus on her exams and pass them.

She hated the police station, and the last time she'd been in there, she'd vowed she'd never return.

"I'm more worried about the news leaking out," Silas said. "You know how things get embellished in the media. With a drug case, I'm not sure your career would survive it, even if the truth comes out later."

Not again. Dread rose in Zora's stomach at the possibility of losing everything she'd worked for. She thought of all the sacrifices she'd made and how everything would be meaningless now.

No! Zora shoved the dread deep down inside and locked it up. This was her life, and no one had the right to steal it. She would get out of this.

Her mom's phone rang. She picked it up, listened, and then ended the call. Her face fell, though she tried to hide it.

"What is it, Mom?" Zora asked.

"The cops have gotten their arrest warrant. They are on their way here."

Zora paced. This was beyond ridiculous. What had she ever done wrong? How had her name ended up linked to a drug dealer? First it was Dave, and now her. What if it was the same person who'd set them up? But why?

She ran her hands through her hair. *Aargh.* But no matter what, she wasn't backing down. Zora just needed more time to find the truth and bring down the monster behind everything. How was she going to get that time?

Silas' phone vibrated. He pulled it out and answered. "What is it?" He listened and then placed the call on speakerphone. "It's Helen. I asked her to monitor the local PD." Helen was an employee at her mother's law firm who worked under Silas. "Helen, Zora and Adrianna are here."

"Hello, Mrs. Smyth, Dr. Smyth."

"Hi, Helen," her mother said. "What's going on?"

"One of the thugs that was arrested for the attempted murder of Dave McKesson made a deal with the cops. He revealed that he'd tailed the mastermind to his hideout after his meeting with their gang leader regarding the bounty on Dave's head. The cops have confirmed the location as an office on Crescent Street. Unfortunately, they found Alisa's business card lying there. The cops are now wondering if Alisa was the one behind the attempt on Dave's life."

"What?" her mom screeched.

"So, they'd like to bring her in for a chat."

"This is ridiculous," Silas said. "Alisa would never do such a thing. First Zora, now Alisa. This is like one big vendetta."

No, not Alisa. All the cops had to do was check into her background, tie her back to the crime family, and that would be the end. They'd judge her before she'd even have a chance.

Zora's heart squeezed in pain. This whole thing was like a venomous gift that kept on giving. Someone was trying to ruin her and her family completely.

"Also…" Helen started. There was more?

"What?" Zora's mom asked.

"Because the Jamie fellow worked across state lines, the Feds are showing an interest in the case. This could end up much bigger than it is now."

Crap, crap, crap. In Zora's opinion, the Feds always made everything three times as bad.

"Thanks for the heads up, Helen. You can get back to work," Silas said.

"Happy to help, sir." She disconnected the line.

How were they going to get out of this mess?

"Alisa, where are you?" Zora hadn't noticed when her mother dialed her number. Her mom had placed it on speakerphone.

"I'm in the office," Alisa said.

"I need you to leave the office and go to the safe house. Can you do that for me?"

"Mom, what's going on?"

"The cops found your business card on Crescent Street, in the office they believe belongs to the mastermind behind the attempt on Dave's life. The cops are going to come looking for you. I need you to disappear for a while until I fix this mess. You know where to go, right?"

"Yes, Mom."

"Good. Go now and stay there. The place has everything you'll need, including a satellite phone. Switch off this phone once this call ends. I'll call you on that line if I need to. The cops are already watching this house, so I can't have you come home yet. But I won't let them take you away from me. I don't believe you had anything to do with this, no matter what anyone says. Can you hear me?"

"Yes, Mom. I'm on my way now."

"Just remember I love you, everyone loves you, and we're fighting for you."

"Thanks, Mom."

"Okay. Bye." The call ended.

Zora had run out of options. She wasn't sure what they could do now. She could see Silas and her mom making calls, trying to stem this tide. But she sensed as surely as her name was Zora, that it was going to be tough to fight against these waves and riptides that threatened to sweep them away.

The enemy thought he'd won.

But there was one door Zora hadn't knocked on, one whose answer may give her what she needed but not what she expected.

She began to pray.

Alisa drove as fast as she could to the safe house without breaking the speed limit. How had it come to this? She'd only wanted to investigate Dave's background. Instead, she'd ended up with a giant target on her forehead.

But how had her card ended up there? She'd finished the old set she had and had only just received this new set with the gold emboss, so she could recall every person whom she'd given them to. She couldn't imagine any of them being the monster behind the attempt on Dave's life.

Then she remembered she'd slipped and fallen in the office at Crescent Street, and her business card had been in her purse at the time.

Had it fallen out then, or had Charles swiped it

while helping her to gather her things? Had everything with him been a pretense, a chance to lure her into his net?

Alisa hit her steering wheel. She'd been a fool. In her bid to prove Dave wrong, she'd been blind to everything else and had ignored the warning signs. Now, she'd only made things worse for herself and her family. She'd been so stupid.

She straightened her shoulders. No, this wasn't the end of the life she'd begun to enjoy.

She didn't know how, but she was going to survive.

And her family was going to make it no matter what.

"Dave, it's bad."

"Tell me, Sean." Sean was one of the newer members on his team at the local PD.

"There's an arrest warrant for Zora because of the testimony of a witness who claimed Zora supplied him prescription pads in exchange for opioid analgesics."

"Zora doesn't do drugs. It's a setup."

"I agree. But that's not even the worst of it. They traced your attempted killer back to an office on Crescent Street and found Zora's sister's card there. They want to question her, too."

This was worse. Alisa's former relationship with the crime family—a connection she'd worked so hard to sever—would get her crucified immediately. It would devastate Zora if anything ever happened to Alisa. She loved her sister with all her heart.

Dave had spent the night mulling over the possible culprits behind the whole fiasco, and now one name burned brighter than the others, especially since Zora had been dragged into this mess.

"Thanks for letting me know, Sean."

"Anytime, man." Dave ended the call.

He dropped the phone on the nightstand and made his way over to the hospital window. Dave felt better today, though the doctor had advised him to take things slowly for now. He looked out: patients, caregivers, and medical staff alike milled around and were enjoying the back gardens or helping someone else enjoy them, despite the slight chill in the air.

Dave closed his eyes and took a deep breath. In his mind, he could smell the chrysanthemums, balloon flowers, and pansies that dotted the landscape.

He admired them for a while, and then he turned and picked up his phone.

Dave knew just what to do. It was the only way to save the situation and make everything right again. The only way to save the woman he loved with all his heart.

He pulled out his phone and dialed the number from memory.

———

"Dave, it's been a long time," the lanky FBI agent with the military crew cut said to him as they shook hands. Dave had met Simon a few years ago while working undercover, and they'd struck up a friendship. They'd lost touch once Dave had moved back to Lexinbridge, but Dave had always known Simon would come running from New York whenever he called for help.

"I know. How's Katie?" Dave asked as he settled back against the pillows behind him on the hospital bed. Katie was Simon's rambunctious daughter.

"She's growing into quite a lady," Simon said, his lips curving into a smile as he pulled up a chair and sat down. Dave could imagine her bossing Simon around.

Then Simon's face turned serious. "What's going on, Dave?"

"I'm ready," Dave replied, though his heart beat faster at the thought of what he was about to do.

For the briefest moment, Simon was confused,

and then he realized what Dave was referring to. His face lit up with excitement. "You mean—"

"Yes."

"This is great news, Dave. I'm glad you finally decided to do this. But are you sure? This is a big deal."

"I'm sure."

Simon's eyes assessed Dave's for a moment and seemed satisfied with what he saw in them. "So, when do you want to leave? I can set everything up as quickly as possible."

"I just need a few hours to tie up some loose ends, and then we can go."

"That works for me."

"But…"

"I knew there had to be a catch. What do you want?"

"I'll do this only on one condition."

"What?"

Dave beckoned Simon closer.

Then he whispered what he wanted.

Zora's eyes fluttered open from the ringing phone. She hadn't realized she'd fallen asleep on the smaller couch in the living room. Even though she'd drawn the curtains, the sun's rays made their way through, though they seemed to burn with less intensity than earlier today. She looked at her watch—it had only been about two hours since she came home.

Silas and her mom sat side by side on the main couch and seemed to have been talking when the call came through.

Silas answered the call. He listened, and then his eyes widened.

"What is it?" her mom asked. He held up his hand

for her to wait while he finished the call. Soon, he tucked his phone back into his pocket.

Silas sat still for a moment, shock written all over his face.

"What is it, Silas?" Her mom shook his arm. "You're scaring me."

He turned to her. "They've dropped the case, Adrianna. Just like that."

Zora sat up. It was over?

"What case? Zora's case? Talk to me."

"Both. It's over."

"How?" Her mom looked more confused than ever.

Zora stood. It was really over! But how?

Silas looked at Zora. Now she could see the sorrow in them.

Her heart rate increased. Why was Silas sad? This had to be bad news.

"I'm sorry, Zora."

"Sorry for what?" Zora asked. By now, her heart pounded in her ears.

"To get the cases dropped and never opened again, Dave went into witness protection."

The gasp that shot out from Zora didn't sound like hers. She felt her chest tighten so hard, like she was about to have a heart attack. *No! It couldn't be. It wasn't right.* Why?

A keening sound tore from her throat as she fell on her knees, the tortured sound like that of an animal that had lost her other half. It blasted from her, filling the space in a never-ending echo.

She felt her mom's arms wrap around her, but still she couldn't stop screaming.

Her heart was torn in two, and somehow she couldn't put it back together again.

Her family was saved, but she'd paid a heavy price for it.

She'd destroyed Dave, just like the nightmare.

EPILOGUE

Alisa still couldn't believe it. The man she'd pushed away and not given a chance had created a miracle. He'd saved both Zora and her.

She'd come home and now sat on the lowest step of the stairs, looking out into the living room, remembering everything, the memories flooding back about the day she'd set eyes on Dave again.

She'd hated him, consumed with a passion to get rid of him from her sister's life.

Instead, he'd chosen to save her, for Zora's sake. Instead of telling her, he'd shown her how much he'd loved Zora, and what it meant to have a big brother, to have a family who cared for her.

Now he was gone, and she would never have the chance to see him again and to thank him.

Zora would always forgive Alisa for what happened, but Alisa wished she didn't have to in the first place.

But she could never roll time back again.

———

The man stared through his binoculars at the police station across the street. He could see the Feds, the men in black suits, milling around.

His jaw tightened. He'd almost made it to the finish line.

He'd set Zora up with the drug dealer. There was no way she should have been able to wriggle out of that situation, which would have destroyed Dave in the worst way possible.

The man had also used Alisa's blinding hate for Dave to entangle her in his web. She'd been so easy to rope in. He'd even allowed the stupid gangbanger to tail him to the temporary office he'd rented just to make it easy for the cops to come after her. A brief check into her background would have sealed the deal.

He'd already started tasting the victory, the rush from destroying his victims that fired him up like no other drug, time and time again.

Then they'd pulled the rug from under him.

He hadn't known Dave and that Smyth family would outfox him.

Now, the Feds were involved, which meant it was time for Charles to take off. They'd been after him for all these years, and even though they were now like a familiar old friend, one mistake was all it would take for them to catch his scent, and it was a risk he couldn't afford.

It was time to disappear.

That Lucas fool would have to deal with the rest on his own.

―――――――

Dave took one step after another as he made his way up the mobile stairway that led up to the plane.

He turned and gazed at the city he was leaving behind. He'd loved this home of his called Lexinbridge, but he would never be back here again.

Dave didn't regret the choice he'd made, though he'd miss Zora with every fiber of his being. He would have to start all over again in an unknown place with a new identity, while hoping and praying the Romanov cartel never caught up with him. But it didn't matter.

Because she was worth it; they were both worth it, and it had been a miracle to have experienced a love like this once in his life. He hoped Zora would be happy and find love again with time.

Even though Dave had no idea where he'd end up, he planned to keep this love he'd experienced close to his heart, letting it warm him on cold days, just like he'd done with another who had died for him.

For Lilianna's sake, the one who'd given her life for his even when he'd made it clear he felt nothing for her except friendship, he'd kept many secrets deep in his heart over all these years, and would have continued to do so if Lucas hadn't tried to hurt those dearest to him.

So it had been time to set them free. Dave had made the deal with the Feds: share his secrets and testify against the Romanov cartel, in exchange for the complete shutdown of the cases against Zora and Alisa, no questions asked. It was a bargain he'd been sure they couldn't resist, and he'd been right.

Now, it was done, and it was time for him to keep his end of the agreement.

Dave took one last look behind him, entered the plane, and watched as the door sealed shut.

———

"Lucas, you have a phone call," the CO said.

Lucas rose to his feet and followed the CO out of the cell and to the warden's office. Maybe today was it, the day he'd finally get the news about Dave's ultimate demise, and about the destruction of the woman who'd been foolish enough to love him.

A few minutes later, he arrived at the office. The warden held out the phone to him, and Lucas collected the receiver and placed it next to his ear. "Hello," he said.

The warden exited the room to give him some privacy.

Lucas listened for a while, then placed the receiver back in the cradle.

He turned, lifted the nearest visitors' chair and smashed it against the wall again and again, where it splintered into a million pieces.

COs rushed into the office at the noise, taking him down and restraining him. But Lucas continued to struggle against them, his strength renewed by the rage that burned in his bitter heart.

He was still muttering and shouting as they carried him out of the office and straight into isolation.

———————

Zora sat on the beach and watched as the waves crashed over each other, over and over, and over again. She hadn't wanted to come this early to view the sunrise, but Brian and Christina had insisted—it was Brian's and Zora's first celebratory moment to mark the end of the board exams.

It had been a wise decision—the air was crisp, the sound of the moving waves calmed her spirit, and the place was empty save for a few early beach regulars. Zora knew it wouldn't be like this in a few more hours, when the place would be teeming with visitors.

She wished Dave was here to enjoy this view with her. A familiar ache swelled in Zora's heart, and she let it crest until it died down. She missed Dave every day, and some days were harder than others, but the goodbye note he'd left, the one the U.S.

Marshals had given to her, had helped. She prayed he was okay wherever he was.

Schyzman and Schyzman had dropped the malpractice suit once the Feds had shut down the drug case. The partners of the firm had done as they'd proposed, and the public apology had helped in smoothing things over at the hospital.

Jamie Tanner, the pharmacy drug dealer, cut a deal with the Feds, but still ended up with a longer sentence than he'd expected.

The final autopsy report had come out as well. Ranitidine, one of the mainstay drugs in the treatment of peptic ulcer, had triggered anaphylaxis in the patient and led to his death.

Clive had made good on his promise. He'd tracked down the real Oliver Young to a rundown motel where he'd been waiting for some smugglers to take him into Mexico. He'd already received some medical care, and his wound had been healing well. His dental records, which AJ and Clive had found, were used to identify him. He also had a mole on his left shoulder, one which the dead body didn't have. Once in custody, Oliver had confessed the truth behind the scam.

Their mother was a gambling addict and had owed the local cartel a lot of money. To redeem her life and cancel her debt, Oliver and Xavier had agreed to the scam. One of the identical twins would present at the ER, while the other would be the one to go into surgery. Then they'd slam the surgeon with a lawsuit for operating on the wrong patient, which would ruin the surgeon's name and career. Since Xavier had been sicker lately, their mother had suggested he'd go in for the actual surgery. That way, he would benefit from the free treatment he'd receive while the case was being settled.

Oliver had shown up first in the ER and then switched with Xavier by the elevators. The bottle of Ranitidine found in the pocket of Xavier's clothes showed he'd taken the second dose right before being wheeled into surgery. But Oliver and his mother hadn't expected Xavier to die—they hadn't counted on a Ranitidine allergy to take his life.

The police arrested the mother, and both she and Oliver had been charged and were awaiting trial.

The mystery client, the man who'd set up the scam and the financier behind the wrongful death lawsuit, had disappeared into the wind and was never found. His money trail had also gone cold—Zora's mom's team had lost its tracks once it'd disappeared into Switzerland.

Zora and her sister had made up, yet she knew it

would take some time before what had transpired didn't hurt as much.

"Zora!"

She turned to see Brian in swim shorts running toward where she and Christina lay on reclining beach chairs. Brian and Christina had reconciled, and Brian had plans to take Christina to meet his parents next week. Zora was just grateful they were happily in love again.

When Brian reached her, his chest heaved as he tried to talk.

Zora chuckled. "We need to get you to the gym," she said. "Just this brief run, and you're already exhausted."

"Mind your business, Zora," Brian said. "Besides, I have more important news for you. I just got the email to check the ABS site for our results!"

"Really?" Christina shrieked.

Zora sat up. The results were out? Her heart thundered in her chest while Christina giggled with excitement beside her. "What are you waiting for?"

"I have some news for you first," he said. "I've heard about the results for some of our colleagues."

There was only one person Zora was interested in. "Herbert?"

Brian shook his head. "Didn't make it."

Zora knew she should be, but she wasn't sorry for him. Herbert had only gotten what was due to him. His precious connections hadn't been able to stop his demise this time around.

"Now, are you ready to check yours?" Brian asked. He held out his tablet to her.

"What about yours?" she asked.

He shook his head. "I haven't checked yet. I need courage from you. You go first."

This was the defining moment for Zora to find out if she was now a board-certified surgeon.

It was time to discover if her dreams had finally come true.

Zora took a deep breath and exhaled. "I'm ready," she said. "Let's do this."

Thank you so much for reading!

Want to know what happens next to Dr. Zora Smyth? You can grab LETHAL RETRACTION at https://dobicross.com

If you've loved reading LETHAL ADHESION, Dobi would be grateful if you could spend a few minutes to leave a review (as short as you like) on the book's page on your favorite retailer. Your review would help bring it to the attention of other readers. Thank you very much.

Check out all Dobi Cross books at
https://dobicross.com

ACKNOWLEDGMENTS

Writing a book is harder and more rewarding than I could have ever imagined. And it would not have been possible without the support, love, and encouragement from my number one cheerleader, my dearest mom. My life would never have been this awesome and wonderful without you.

Of course, I have to thank my precious little DC for his smiles and antics. You brighten my day and give me the strength to keep pushing through.

Thank you to my sisters for encouraging me on this wonderful journey. And a special thanks to my baby brother (who is so not a baby anymore) for being super supportive and checking in on my progress. You guys are the best.

Thank you to my wonderful author friends. You know who you are. Your selflessness and willingness to share what you know has made my writing journey smoother and an exciting one. And a special thanks to Lisa and Deanna whose support have made a difference.

Most of all, I want to thank God who gave me life, surrounded me with the most wonderful people, and loved me all the way. You make my life complete.

And finally, a special thanks to all my readers whose love of my stories spur me on to write more. Thank you!

ABOUT THE AUTHOR

As a former physician and business executive in another life—with a childhood filled with reading multi-genre novels (including Shakespeare in the original version)—Dobi Cross loves to write thrilling stories with heart.

She enjoys dreaming up everyday characters who rise above unfavorable circumstances to overcome incredible odds. When not writing, Dobi can be found binging K-dramas and ice cream with her little sidekick by her side.

Lethal Adhesion is the fifth book in the Dr. Zora Smyth Medical Thriller Series. Sign up at https://dobicross.com to be notified when the next Dobi Cross book comes out!

Thanks for reading LETHAL ADHESION!

https://dobicross.com
hello@dobicross.com
facebook.com/dobicrossauthor
bookbub.com/profile/dobi-cross
instagram.com/dobicross